LAURA VOGT (Teufen, 1989) studied Creative Writing at the Swiss Literature Institute in Biel and Cultural Studies at the University of Luzern. Her first novel *So einfach war es zu gehen* came out in 2016. She has also written numerous short stories and articles as well as lyrical and dramatic texts. Laura started writing *What Concerns Us* two months after having her first child. This is her second novel and the first one to be available to English readers.

CAROLINE WAIGHT is an award-winning literary translator working from Danish, German and Norwegian. She translates both fiction and non-fiction, with recent publications including *The Lobster's Shell* by Caroline Albertine Minor (Granta, 2022), *Island* by Siri Ranva Hjelm Jacobsen (Pushkin Press, 2021) and *The Chief Witness* by Sayragul Sauytbay & Alexandra Cavelius (Scribe, 2021)

Laura Vogt

What Concerns Us

TRANSLATED FROM THE GERMAN
BY CAROLINE WAIGHT

HÉ/OÏSE

PRESS

First published in English in Great Britain in 2022 by
Héloïse Press Ltd
4 Pretoria Road
Canterbury CT1 1QL
www.heloisepress.com

First published under the original German language title *Was uns betrifft*
© 2020 Zytglogge, Switzerland

This translation © Caroline Waight 2022

Cover design by Laura Kloos
Copy-edited by Robina Pelham Burn
Text design and typesetting by Tetragon, London
Printed and bound in Great Britain by CPI Group (UK) Ltd, Croydon, CR0 4YY

With the support of the Swiss Arts Council Pro Helvetia

ISBN 978-1-7397515-1-7

Prologue

Verena drew the checked shirt over her head and placed it on the kitchen chair. Taking hold of her waistband, left and right, she slipped off her cotton trousers and her knickers; then, shivering, she opened the pantry and reached for the cognac. Quickly she pulled the cork and took five gulps, feeling the warmth spread in her belly. She filled half a cup, poured the shimmering golden fluid into a bowl, cracked five eggs and added the yolks, dropping the whites into the now-empty cup. She stirred the mixture of cognac and yolk with a wooden spoon, then picked up the bowl, carried it into the bathroom and set it on the floor. Shaping her hand into a trowel, she dipped it into the oozy mass and massaged it carefully through her greying brown hair. She'd been letting it grow out these past few months, and by now it reached her earlobes. The mass was cool. It dripped onto her shoulders, her chest, onto the floor. Verena shovelled until the bowl was empty, then she pulled herself upright, holding onto the basin, braced herself with both hands and looked into the mirror as a yellowish runnel trickled slowly down her forehead to her nose. A sweet, sharp odour. Verena gazed rigidly into her own eyes. She was stock still until the timer in the kitchen began to beep five minutes later, a shrill tone that grew ever quicker and shorter. Climbing into the tub, she ran the hot water. Tuft after tuft of hair swilled down into the drain with the cognac and egg. Verena turned off the tap and grabbed a towel to dry her feet, her thighs, her stomach; she worked her way up until she reached her nearly bald head. Then, wrapping the towel around her waist, she went back into the kitchen. Her skin glowed as she switched off the timer, lit the hob and slid the egg whites into a frying pan with a squirt of oil. She ate the scrambled whites with her hands, standing, straight from the pan.

PART ONE

I

On the day an egg left her right ovary and attached itself to a sperm cell, compelled by luteinising hormone, Rahel was at a reading, second row from the front. The piece was about a protagonist named Boris who had built a house of glass in a remote Swiss village near the German border, and there was a tickle between Rahel's legs whenever her gaze fell on the author's light-brown topknot. When she briefly closed her eyes she heard his dark, firm voice. Observing him in profile, she'd never have put him at nearly forty, as the programme said he was. He looked determined, gazing down at his book. Fiery. He seemed to burn with every word he read aloud, but as soon as he raised his eyes the expression faded, as though he realised the piece wasn't right for the audience. Again and again he narrowed his eyes. Not a handsome man, thought Rahel, as she continued to examine him, with his long torso bowing into a slack C and his button-up shirt taut across his navel. And yet she felt desire, while at the same time, unnoticed, a male and a female pronucleus were merging into a single cell inside her, destined to begin dividing the next day, making their way towards her womb at a slow and steady pace. The cluster of cells would embed into the rich uterine lining, making Rahel's breasts swell. In the first few days after conception, after the reading at the literary festival, her head would clear; only her body would sense the novelty, the unfamiliarity: this unborn. Rahel would wander through those late spring days as though wound in cotton wool, chewing fresh leaves from the rosemary growing on her balcony while Billie Holiday's voice poured like warm wax through her headphones into her ears and she sang along out loud.

The heat came earlier than the meteorologists had forecast. Eighteen days after the reading, on 5 July, Rahel was in her stuffy practice room by half past seven, gazing at a score covered in scribbles. Last night's concert hadn't gone well: her stomach had rebelled, as though there wasn't enough room for it, and her diaphragm had felt weak. During the fast passages her voice had kept cracking. Rahel had lain awake long into the night, and in the morning she'd forgotten to comb her hair. A strand fell across her forehead, and she tucked it back behind her ear again and again with her left hand. She couldn't make sense of the notes anymore. Her body pumped blood ceaselessly into her head, much too much and much too fast; she shifted her weight from one leg to the other. In her right hand she clasped the pregnancy test she'd taken half an hour earlier. The two pink lines flashed in her mind's eye, warning lights that grew rounder and rounder, turning into ovals, and inside them eye, eye, nose, mouth: one brightly lit face and one in shadow, her mother, her father, Verena, Erik.

Rahel began to sing, but her voice sounded husky and kept skidding on the high notes. The faces came apart, plunging into the place between light and shadow, into the absence that had engulfed them both for a long time, in very different ways.

Rahel picked up her phone, which she'd set to one side on the folding table, next to an apple with a bite taken out. She still felt like throwing up. *Hyperemesis* was the first word she googled, followed by *genitals*, *conception*, *pregnancy*. That morning Rahel called these things exclusively by their scientific names. *Oocyte*, *spermatozoon*, *ovary*, *tube*, *embryology*. She tried to reconstruct the history of the conception: *luteinising hormone*, *diploid sister-chromatid set*, *uterus*. Words that orbited her like distant planets, and so she sang the terms, wrapped in shrill, haphazard melodies.

Seven months after the nucleus implanted, at the book launch of a well-known Zurich-based author, she recognised amid the crowd that light-brown hair tied back into a bun. The topknot clung to the back of his head like a tiny sun. He was in the foyer, leaning against a balustrade, his left foot on the bottom step and a glass of white wine in his right hand. Rahel walked up to him, and without a word of greeting she began to speak, to talk about Boris from the book. She'd felt close to him, not just at the event a few months earlier but while reading at home.

I would fall in love with him, she said. With the Boris in your book.

Pleasure to meet you. Boris, he said, and held out his free hand.

His expression wasn't quite as Rahel remembered, his eyes less round, more piercing than from afar. She took a step backwards.

Isn't your name Wolf?

He held out his glass to her.

I haven't drunk from it yet, he said. I'll get a beer. Hang on.

He turned away and made for the buffet. Rahel looked into the glass in her hands; the neon lighting made the wine look like lemonade. Moments later, Boris was back. He raised his beer bottle.

Wolfgang is my given name, he said. Wolf Knupp's what I write under. My friends call me Boris. My middle name.

I'm Rahel, she said, holding out her hand.

He gave it a short, firm squeeze.

What did you think of the reading? he asked.

Rahel shrugged.

It was alright, she said.

Yeah, same, he replied. Well written, but nothing beyond that yet. All smooth, shiny surface.

I know what you mean, said Rahel. She let a finger flick against her wine glass, and a bright note rang out. There's no openness about it, she went on. No space.

He took a sip of beer and glanced at the label.

Are you working on anything new? she asked.

Writing for me is always something ongoing. I can be wall-papering, sitting on the train, holding a pen, whatever – it happens. So, yes, I've got something in the works.

He turned his head a little to the side and grazed his fingers over his topknot.

And you, do you write as well? he asked.

Lyrics, said Rahel, and told him about training to become a singer, and how her life since she left music school consisted of finding sounds – or rather, finding a sound of her own.

Yellow, said Boris.

Rahel rested a hand on her waist and smiled.

14

I don't sing soprano.

Jazz, then? That'd work with the yellow.

Most people can't tell that about me, said Rahel. I look too much of a goody two-shoes. That's what my sister says, anyway.

For yellow?

For jazz. And your sound? Green, blue?

I've given up on sound, said Boris. I tell stories. They're about content, full stop.

And polishing the language?

Language is a means to an end. It's a way into the story that was in my head – for other people, too.

I don't believe you. There's no extravagant language in your novel, sure, but there's something behind it. Or underneath it. I really liked that.

Boris took a few more sips of his beer. As though he'd only just noticed it, he eyed Rahel's belly.

When are you due? he asked, carefully taking the wine glass from her hands. He threw her a mischievous look before downing it in one gulp.

Soon, she said. Will you take me?

Where?

To the hospital.

He laughed out loud and put the empty wine glass on the stairs.

What about the man in your life? he asked.

South America.

Were you travelling?

He went travelling as soon as he found out he was going to be a dad.

He ditched you?

You might say that.

Must be a great guy.

Nah, it's an old story. Husband and family, it never works out.

Really? asked Boris.

I can think of a million examples, Rahel said. My dad left too, when my mum got pregnant with my little sister. Open door, close door, buh-bye.

I'm sorry. But still. There are at least as many families where living together does work out.

Boris paused for a moment.

Is it really so easy for you to tar all men with the same brush? he asked.

No, she said. But one thing is pretty clear to me. Fathers don't stick around.

Boris looked directly at Rahel, his expression soft now, downy hair barely visible over his thick stubble. Unblinking, he said: Fine, I'll take you. To the hospital.

Rahel shrank back, putting her thumb and index finger to her left earlobe.

Are there any non-alcoholic ones? she asked, after a short, electric silence.

What?

Beers.

I don't think so.

Maybe at the Asian place next door, said Rahel. Want to come and see?

Why not? Boris said.

In the months before, the baby had granted Rahel a peaceful pregnancy, at least physically. The movements in her belly had felt soft and flowing. The first major examination in her thirteenth week revealed an active little creature. Rahel lay on a hard couch while the doctor put a dollop of gel on her exposed stomach and pressed the ultrasound wand into it. On a screen attached to the wall, Rahel watched as the creature stretched its fingers, put a thumb to its mouth, then turned away.

A lively foetus, the doctor had said.

What else would it be? wondered Rahel on the way home through the streets of Bern, Schneeweiss und Rosenrot's 'Daddy Longleg' in her ear, a song she had listened to many times before. Drums, piano and double bass mingled with the squeal of the passing trams, but the singer's voice felt very close, as though it were coming from Rahel's own head. The doctor's words had left her feeling awkward. Lively. What had she meant by that? Spirited, cheerful, vivacious? That sounded just like Fenna. Apparently her sister wasn't the only one more delighted with the life in her belly than she was – so was the doctor. She had been expecting someone sober, someone who wouldn't pass comment on the foetus. The doctor's gaiety had been in stark contrast to the medical jargon. *Posterior placenta*, *portio*, *prenatal diagnosis*.

My foetus, said Rahel softly, as she stopped at Viktoriaplatz and fished the ultrasound images out of her jacket pocket. Although she'd decided to dump them straight into the nearest bin, she took another look. Set against the greyish plane that apparently represented her uterine wall was a creature, ghostly, with a clearly recognisable brain in the shape of a heart. During the consultation, the doctor had explained exactly what was what. The head, the nuchal fold, the thighs and the little feet: everything was measured, saved on the computer and finally given a verbal tick – 'within normal range'. The pictures disgusted Rahel, and in turn she felt ashamed. Children and the stage were antonyms, that seemed quite clear to her. Either/or. And the child had already decided for her. Switching off the music, she pulled the headphones out of her ears.

In the weeks that followed, Rahel's belly started to balloon, and the bigger it got the calmer she felt. The nausea subsided. The foetus was becoming a child. The uterus a womb. The placenta nourishment. Words like flashcards, matching like for like as Rahel turned them over, and the connection between these terms and the real thing, the creature in her belly, began haltingly to emerge, little by little. But there was nothing to be done about the child's almost non-existent connection to its biological father. She had never been close to him, except for the physical attraction. A brief affair, pregnant despite a condom.

Sounds more like me than you, Fenna had remarked with a grin when Rahel told her, and she had answered: Maybe we're not as different as you always think.

I don't think anything, Fenna had replied, taking a long drag on her cigarette.

At least her child would be beautiful: a boy, Rahel was sure, who looked like his father. Rahel pictured Martin's face, his freckles, the curly dark-blond hair she had loved to run through her fingers. She liked Martin's hulking frame and hoped her son would take after him in that regard instead of her.

She still got queasy when she went into the kitchen and saw the portrait of Eve by Albrecht Dürer tacked to the fridge. Rahel's ex-boyfriend Chris had sent it to her a few months earlier, along with a piece of paper on which he had scrawled the word *sinner* in thick felt-tip pen. She had cheated on him with Martin. The sight of the capital letters had made her laugh out loud. Schoolboy handwriting. She'd chucked the note into the wastepaper bin and left the picture on the kitchen table. From then on, though, the more she looked at it, over her morning coffee, her lunchtime salad, her dinner, the more it started to hurt. Suddenly she was struck by her resemblance to Eve: the milky, almost gleaming skin, the questioning, critical, yet somewhat lost look, and above all the narrow, sloping shoulders. After two weeks she put the picture up on the fridge with a magnet and finally made an appointment with the dressmaker to order a tailored blazer with shoulder pads. She wanted to cancel out once and for all the shoulders she had hated even as a child.

After she had found out she was carrying a baby, Rahel had tried again and again to convince herself that Eve in Hebrew wasn't the sinner but the animator, the bringer of life. Her body was shaping another, a new body. Her body was growing beyond itself. At the same time, she became even more withdrawn. She no longer felt the urge for strong coffee and hard bread for breakfast, or for the hours of rehearsals, the conversations with bandmates and former fellow students on her narrow balcony, for wiping off black eyeliner at night.

In retrospect, Rahel couldn't say why she'd seized responsibility for her child so vehemently, even early on in the pregnancy, and without ever really considering other options, including when it came to Martin. Every night she'd swallowed lumpen words such as 'money' and 'education'. They were indigestible. How was she supposed to be a mother? She saw Verena, standing in the doorway like a wax figure at Madame Tussauds, only her mouth moving: I've got to work, my girl, or we won't make ends meet.

For a few seconds they had stood face to face, eleven-year-old Rahel with her tousled hair and Verena in her mannish clothes and short crop.

Then Rahel had snivelled the snot back up her nose and replied: Why can't you just find yourself a new husband?

Now, twenty-seven and pregnant, Rahel was sure of one thing: she wouldn't do anything like Verena. She would always be there for her child, no matter what. But she knew her patchy income wouldn't be enough for two, not in the long run: the couple of gigs with her band, the weekend job at a café and the weekday shifts at the supermarket didn't bring in much. The thought of looking for a permanent job as a singing teacher or going back to the library made her shudder. Rahel cancelled all her upcoming concerts. She crept into bed, read articles about motherhood and modern ways of bringing up a child, and sometimes she scrolled through job portals, though without looking closely at any particular ad. Later, she would remember the precise moment in her seventeenth week, months before she met Boris, when she suddenly jumped out of bed, exhilarated, stood there on solid legs and felt alive with joy: she was going to be a mother; she was going to find a father.

2

On the night of 24 March, as Rahel was washing the salad, she felt a powerful tug in her belly. False, false, false labour, she thought each time the pain momentarily brought her breathing to a standstill. Putting her hand on the small of her back, she smiled at Boris as he laid out plates, cutlery, salad and bread. Finally sitting opposite one another, they forked down wilted leaves and viscous dressing. Then they listened to hits from Rahel's childhood and teenage years on YouTube: 'Lemon Tree', 'Macarena', 'I'll Be Missing You'. She looked alternately from Puff Daddy singing in a grass-green meadow to Boris, bobbing his head to the music and washing down every bite with a sip of beer. Neither of them said a word, but Rahel kept bursting into fits of laughter. Boris watched her, chewing.

What is it? he asked, once he'd emptied his plate.

Rahel shrugged.

Nothing, she said.

After they'd washed up Boris retreated into his room, while Rahel roamed around the house and tidied, the first time since moving in with him three weeks after they met. He had told Rahel about his house in Eastern Switzerland that first evening, after they left the book launch together and ordered sweet jasmine tea at a Thai takeaway because there was no alcohol-free beer.

It's remote, not far from a small town called Gesswil, on a slope. From the house you can see a few fruit trees, and beyond them the forest. It's an old farmhouse with an adjoining barn, although there haven't been any animals in it for years, and I'm going to convert it, I want to turn it into a big studio. The house has three floors, seven rooms, low ceilings. Homely. And best of all: when the wind blows hard you can hear it inside. The house shivers.

Did you grow up there? asked Rahel.

Boris shook his head.

I inherited it from my aunt three years ago. At the time I was planning to move to Italy for a while, but then things just happened. I gave notice at my flat in Zurich and spent most of my time at the house, writing and renovating. When I'm in Zurich I can stay with a friend.

Boris paused.

To be honest, that happens less and less often. I don't miss the city.

As she listened, Rahel stroked with one finger the colourful bunch of flowers printed on the teacup. She liked Boris's deep, solid voice and the strangely contrary sense of easing into him when she raised her head and looked into his face, at his soft cheeks, his strong nose and his eyes, which were steadily but gently fixed on her.

I could happily do without the city too, she said.

So why are you still here?

When I first got pregnant I was panicking a bit. I couldn't afford my flat in Bern, and I just happened to end up at Maya's. I'm only staying with her temporarily.

Do you work here in Zurich?

I haven't worked at all for several weeks now.

You've chucked it in, the music stuff?

Soon there won't be room for it anyway.

Why not? asked Boris.

Juggling kids, work and music? Doubt there's much chance of that.

Isn't singing your job?

A job to me is a way of earning money. Singing is something I've done forever. But I did do an apprenticeship as an information and documentation assistant when I was sixteen. I was a media manager at a library. That made it possible to move out of my mother's place early on, because the job was in Zurich. After that I was able to finance my studies at the jazz school in Bern.

Rahel brushed a hand across her forehead and looked at Boris.

There's no way I'm going back to the library, she went on. I've been putting some money aside. Shall we get something to eat?

Will you be paying with a live show?

I'm not that short of cash just yet, said Rahel, leaning back.

Around half-ten, despite Rahel's fervent protests, Boris paid for the tea and the meal as well as the taxi that took them home, first her then him. Before she got out, he asked her if they could meet up again, and Rahel said yes, and ten days later she also agreed, after a moment's hesitation, when he asked if she wanted to move into his house.

It had been one of those spring-like February days. They had gone ambling through the streets for ages, searching for one of

Zurich's green spaces. Rahel and her already sizeable belly had to keep sitting down – on park benches, at restaurant tables, on steps; she leant against Boris again and again as they walked. He didn't ask her about the past. She felt free to talk about what mattered to her, about her work, about her thoughts on music. She was surprised how well Boris understood her, her way of working, which was different from his – he worked more cautiously than she did, but more consistently, while her creativity had always manifested itself in fits and starts. As they sat on a bench near the Botanical Gardens, Rahel told him about Martin, who had spawned the baby in her belly. He didn't actually live in South America but in Vienna, and he wanted nothing more to do with her or the child.

Vienna and Rome, both jinxed, said Boris, and described in terse sentences his relationship with the woman who had almost made him emigrate to Abruzzo. He'd got to know Anna during a six-month stay in the Italian capital, part of a grant he'd been awarded. At the end of the six months Boris had returned to Zurich to pack his things, when out of the blue she'd broken up with him, over the phone. Something wasn't right, Anna had sobbed into the receiver, Boris had pushed her too hard. Better to forget about building a family together.

Realising Boris was already taken, Rahel felt a short, fierce pang. Her legs had gone to sleep, and she tapped them awake with the heels of her hands.

Everything I wrote in Rome, Boris continued, I threw out. Too immoderate, too quick. I relied on older material for the novel and eventually finished it in Gesswil.

Do you still think about Anna much? asked Rahel.

No. But sometimes there's a shadow.

They were silent, Rahel stretching one leg after the other and looking at Boris, whose attention seemed to be caught by something across the street. Erik, her own father, flitted through her head; she saw him vaguely in her mind's eye, and caught herself searching for similarities with Boris. He had to be about the same height, but broader, his hair darker; he was nothing like the man in the few photos Rahel had seen of Erik. Only that expression, the way Boris gazed absently into the distance, reminded Rahel of a photograph: herself as a baby in her father's arms, him facing the camera but with an aimless look; Erik had been far away even then.

I'm building a place for literature, you're looking for a place for music, said Boris, interrupting Rahel's thoughts. It's a good fit.

More than anything I need a place for this baby, said Rahel, tracing small circles on her belly with her hands.

A woman sauntered past in high-heeled boots. Once the clacking of her shoes had died away, Boris asked: Move in with me in Gesswil?

He turned his face to hers. It shone with a pale lustre.

You can stay as long as it suits us both. We'll form a community. As friends.

Rahel unclasped her hands, spread her fingers and examined them for a moment.

What do you want in return? Sex with a pregnant lady?

She gave a laugh.

Are you being serious? asked Boris.

Your offer is too generous, Rahel said.

I've got plenty of space. You need space. The equation is balanced, it's that simple.

Life is never that simple.

Would you like a few days to think it over?

No. Let's give it a shot.

Yeah, I think we should as well.

As she went through the house, moving from one room to the next, her contractions escalated. Rahel kept stopping to breathe deeply in and out. In her study she came across the only cardboard box she hadn't unpacked since the move. Opening the lid, she ran her hand over the letters she'd received during her apprenticeship and student days: letters from her mother, from Fenna. While Fenna always filled several pages, Verena's had consisted of two or three words of greeting and a newspaper article: articles about singers studying at one of the music colleges in Switzerland, about musicians from the USA, from England; articles about concerts in Bern or Zurich that she thought might interest Rahel. They did, definitely, although Rahel rarely answered Verena's letters, and they saw each other even less. Fenna often met up with Rahel, both during and after her studies, but she only saw Verena when Fenna was there too. Fenna, the beautiful, free-spirited sister she had always envied, and not just for her figure. She had curving hips and broad thighs, but they didn't make her look heavy, far from it. Despite her ample body she seemed weightless, her bearing upright, her blonde, gently curling hair bouncing over her shoulders; on her feet, which were relatively small for her height, she usually wore low-cut shoes.

Rahel picked up an envelope and placed it on the desk, breathing into a contraction. Sitting down on the floor, she leant her back against the wall. The window aslant from her was luminous; a full moon. A vast heat was spreading from her belly throughout her body, her head was packed in cotton wool and her surroundings lost their contours; objects melded into one, the desk became part of the window, the window flowed into the wall, the wall was a cratered landscape of shadows, pits and furrows, and Rahel's body was the only constant in the room, the centre of a rotating universe. Getting onto all fours, she moved her pelvis in circles, but that only made the pain worse. The urge to use the toilet overwhelmed her. She picked herself up, walking slowly, setting foot after foot, through the study and the dark corridor and into the bathroom. Nothing but a thin trickle of urine dripped into the bowl. Rahel pulled her knickers and trousers back up, lay down on the bathroom mat and stared at the white ceiling above. Deep inside her was a small vibrating piece of heated iron, which began to ring: a buzzing peal.

Later, she couldn't say how much time she'd spent in the bathroom. But she remembered that the pain had changed at some point, become more oppressive but less extreme. Rahel clambered back up, grabbed the window handle and pulled herself upright, one hand resting on her lower back. Opening the window, she inhaled the cool March air and the scent of snow on the way. Into the cold, loud and clear, she shrieked her first real contraction into being. She came round only when the second one seized her whole body, and suddenly she saw Boris's face in front of hers, his drowsy stare.

He called the hospital and said they were on their way, then put Rahel into her winter coat and took her to the car. She lay down on the back seat, but as soon as Boris started the car she screamed that the baby was coming now, it was already there, she could feel it.

Slipping her hand into her pyjamas, she felt a tuft of hair. She stroked the soft mop as she tried to ease her contractions. She was the child, and the child was her. The stretch in her belly was not unpleasant; the baby's head filled every centimetre, she was completely in the moment. She kept seeing a moving image: her arm outstretched, sweeping, her clenched fist opening to scatter little seeds that sailed to the ground and began to sprout before they even landed in the grass, turning into orange-coloured blossoms.

In the delivery room it took two minutes and two contractions, then Rico was born.

Rahel kept slurring, as though drunk: It's you. It's you.

The same day, after a few hours' rest at the hospital, the three of them went home. Softly humming Nancy Wilson's 'Can't Take My Eyes Off You', Rahel walked into the house. There, before Rico's birth, she had sometimes dreamt she had to board a ship, one that took her to some unknown port, to people who didn't speak her language. Here, in this house, she had said a wordless goodbye to the world she had once known: Bern, Zurich, her life on and near the stage. All of it was dream-fogged and far away. Boris's house was a new world, Rahel could sense that quite clearly now as she went upstairs to her bedroom, holding Rico in her arms. Getting into bed with the baby on her stomach, she gazed up at the low wooden ceiling and was happy.

Six weeks after the birth, Rahel slept with Boris for the first time. As soon as Rico had dozed off on the sheepskin in the living room, they drew towards each other, as though it were the obvious thing to do; Boris's tongue felt familiar in Rahel's mouth, and she let him take her into his bedroom, let herself be absorbed back into desire. Her skin was a shimmering membrane. She put her hands on Boris's face and slid them over his neck, his chest, his stomach, his penis, his thighs, when suddenly she heard Rico babble, howl and instantly go quiet again. For a second she hesitated, tempted to pull away from Boris and rush into the living room, pick Rico up; but she stayed, and that aroused her even more. She bore down on Boris with her full weight.

She was astonished by her orgasm. It didn't feel like masturbation had towards the end of her pregnancy, when a twitching warmth had filled her abdomen from clitoris to ribs. The feeling that it triggered above the pubic bone was more concentrated, but more intense.

When Boris and Rahel finally drew apart, Rico began to whimper again, raising his voice and shouting more loudly. Boris got up and left the room naked. Seconds later he came back with the boy in his arms, wrapped in a woollen blanket. One corner of the blanket swung back and forth, like Boris's penis, back and forth; he walked with his head held high, like a Roman legionary, thought Rahel. Almost as soon as Rico was lying in front of her, Boris behind her, the boy started crying again; Rahel gave him her right breast and he began to nurse. She wished she could have captured the image: her two men surrounding her, caring for her, and her caring for them in return. She used a cloth to dab away the drops of milk that pearled from her left breast.

From then on, every day, Rahel tied her son into a sling, took Boris's hand and went for a walk. She hummed to herself, even while she was breastfeeding Rico, bathing with him, accompanying him into sleep. Her eyes were softly and unswervingly fixed on him, and he wanted only to keep slurping at her breasts.

Rahel said the baby needed a mother, warmth and milk, nothing else. Nothing else yet. Visitors, already few and far between, became increasingly rare.

Boris's parents had reacted with outrage to the news that a woman had moved into his house, heavily pregnant but not by him. Rahel could scarcely contain her laughter as Boris stood there in the kitchen and imitated his small, wiry mother, putting on her voice and crossing his arms, parroting her opinion that parents had to leave each child half a million Swiss francs or they were putting the continued existence of the Swiss state at risk. His mother believed that, as a writer, he relied on exploiting the system, so he had no right to a family.

Boris shook himself off, brushed the hair from his face and put his arm around Rahel.

Awful, he said, and took a long swig of beer.

Rahel didn't tell Boris much about her own parents. He was aware she had a fractured relationship with Verena, who lived in Aargau in the north of Switzerland – much like he did with his mother, but for different reasons. He knew her father had walked out on his family when she was a little girl. Like Rico's biological father, Rahel's had gone travelling. Emigrated, she said. Since then she'd had one solitary sign of life, during her student days. The letter must have been posted in Asia or South America, thought Rahel, because her father had been in a country that began with the letter P, and she listed them for him: Paraguay or Peru, the Philippines or Pakistan. Or Peking.

Peking is a city.

My father needed a lot of space. Peking is nearly seventeen thousand square kilometres – that ought to be enough for him, Rahel said.

She barely remembered Erik. But one scene did resurface in her mind every couple of months: she heard the deafening bang of a door slammed shut, and felt a chill begin to creep through her childhood home, as though the walls had abruptly turned to ice. Rahel, too, had turned to ice, and her lump-of-ice fingers couldn't finish buttoning the white Sunday dress of the doll on the bed in front of her. She stood there baffled, gripping the doll's hard plastic shoulders. It wasn't until a few minutes later – when Rahel heard her mother crying, softly at first, then louder and louder until it turned into a wail – that she broke out of her daze. The ice in her body melted and splashed her legs. She took a few steps out of her room and saw Verena pacing up and down the narrow hall, her hands on her big belly. When she reached the door of the flat she hammered it three times with her fists, turned around, went up, down. It was a while before she noticed Rahel standing in the doorway.

She screamed: You've wet yourself, what are you thinking? Get changed right now!

Peking or Pyongyang, Paramaribo or Panama, said Rahel. No one knows.

A few weeks after he disappeared, when Rahel was five and a half and Verena was seven months pregnant, Erik sent a single postcard. Verena burned it solemnly with a lighter on the little balcony, then lit a hand-rolled cigarette and took a few deep drags.

Let's just hope the kid in here doesn't turn out to be a boy. Verena pointed at her belly.

I'd like to a have a brother, Rahel said.

You can go and look for a brother and a father somewhere else, Verena retorted sharply.

When is Daddy coming back?

He isn't. He doesn't want a girl and he doesn't want a woman.

Doesn't he like me? asked Rahel almost inaudibly.

No, Verena said, I really don't think he does.

She laid one hand on her belly and put the trembling cigarette to her mouth with the other. Then she stubbed it out on the railing and the wind carried off the ashes, like the ashes of the postcard.

We'll be a women's shelter, the three of us, Verena said decisively, getting to her feet and walking into the flat without turning back.

Unable to move, Rahel stayed on the balcony, flanked by a bulging sack of rubbish and a clothes horse draped with socks, and her lips narrowed as though of their own accord, cutting in half the words she had begun to unfurl with the tip of her tongue. What she had left were notes, and she gently hummed a tune to herself.

Verena turned out to be right. Not long afterwards she gave birth to another girl, her little hussy, as she put it. Fenna.

The simple jazz melodies that Rahel hummed after Rico's birth interwove as time went on into polyphony. Her compositions had developed this way since childhood. Whenever she ducked into her study for fifteen minutes after Rico had fallen asleep, she jotted down the melodies on music paper. She no longer wrote any lyrics. Her new perspective on the world, the fact of being a mother, could not be expressed in words. When Rico was seven months old the melodies faded too, leaving blood-less student words behind them: *dissonance, polyrhythm, changes*. Rahel put the scores she'd written into the bin. She'd known it. Singing was history.

Boris was content with his study in the attic, and his plan to convert the barn was shelved. Day after day he worked on his novel. He'd read excerpts from it to Rahel on her second night in Gesswil: a surreal tale set in the Roman Empire. Like the one she was already familiar with, these excerpts were polished, beautifully worded, and revealed their mystery only at a second glance. From then on, when she thought of the house of glass, she saw not Boris the character behind the panes but her Boris, whose first name was Wolfgang. He was seated in an armchair reading the paper, with a heap of stones beside him. All he had to do was bend down and throw, thought Rahel.

From time to time Boris worked as a freelance journalist or as a German teacher at a small language school, always as much and as long as was necessary, which meant until he had scraped together enough money that he didn't have to think about earning any more for a few months. For bigger expenses, he had his aunt's inheritance put aside.

Rahel cooked, cleaned, worked in the garden, pickled vegetables, played with Rico and cuddled up with him in bed after lunch. Long after Rico had stopped breastfeeding, she continued to refuse Boris's repeated suggestions that he look after Rico in the afternoons to give her time for music.

I'm living a family life now, and if that's what I'm going to do, then I'll do it right, Rahel said that evening on the sofa.

Boris, sprawled next to her, shrugged. To be honest, I'd really like to spend a bit more time alone with Rico. It would do us all good.

Things suit me just fine as they are right now.

And you don't care what suits me?

You don't have to take on that responsibility. We talked about this before Rico was born, Rahel said.

But I want to. We're a family now, aren't we?

Rahel wrapped her arms around Boris's neck.

Yes. And I want to be a good wife to you, she said.

Boris pulled away.

Stop it, he said.

Stop being a good wife to you?

34

Rahel stifled a laugh.

Stop acting like I'm the one demanding you take care of everything in such a self-sacrificing way. Cleaning the kitchen once a week is enough, it doesn't have to be every day. And a few bruised vegetables in the fridge aren't the end of the world. You don't always have to be running around putting them in jars.

What are you trying to say?

You always want to control everything. Take a step back.

Rahel frowned.

I'm well aware that I'm not Rico's biological dad. Which is fine. But don't you realise how obvious you always make that?

Rahel shook her head very slightly.

Don't begrudge us our afternoons, Boris said.

And what am I supposed to do with the time?

Sing. Write. Or start hanging out with friends again. Grab a coffee in the city.

I don't need that stuff anymore.

How can you turn your back on it, just like that? Especially music.

Singing for me was always about saying goodbye, Rahel said. And now I'm here.

And writing?

Family is enough for me, she said. I've got to concentrate.

He adjusted his cushion.

Sometimes I feel like you want me for yourself but not for Rico, he said.

Rahel turned to look at him.

You're wrong. You are his father. And I want at least six more kids with you.

She straightened up and went on: Let's start with one. I'm sure it will bring us together properly. As a family.

Boris flashed a clenched smile that made the bones in his jaw stand out.

Rahel slipped her hand into his waistband.

Are you sure? asked Boris.

Definitely, she said. Children with your eyes, your mouth.

She slid her hand further down. I want you, you, you.

She undid the button, undid the zip, pulled his trousers off.

And what do you want? she whispered.

Climbing back on top of Boris, she focused on his face.

Now you want me, don't you?

Sure, a bit.

A bit?

Boris cupped her neck gently with both hands.

Something's really got to give, Rahel.

Yes, she said. I understand.

Putting his hands on her breasts, she asked: And you're the kind of man who sticks around, right?

Boris nodded.

3

Sometimes I dream of gaps, said Fenna. It was early summer. She sat at the kitchen table, watching Luc break three eggs and put them in a plastic bowl.

I'm fascinated by the in-between. Landscapes that are uninhabited, or barely inhabited, for instance. At some point I'd like to go and live on an isolated farm in the Jura Mountains, where the Doubs winds deep into the gorge. There'll be some sort of ancient forest between my house and the river. I'll fight my way through the dense undergrowth, and when I reach the bottom I'll plunge face-first into the glittering water, reach out and grab a fish with my bare hands, then take it home and roast it for dinner.

Luc laughed, his muscles tensing as he raised his arm, briefly touched her hand and said she was a romantic, and yeah sure, they'd go hiking along the Doubs one day. Or climbing.

He grabbed the whisk and mixed the eggs, milk and onions. The oil hissed in the pan. Luc poured them in.

Definitely, said Fenna. Soon.

She filled Luc's wine glass almost to the brim and pushed it towards him.

The mountains would be lovely. Or we could go up to the Bosco d'Öss, said Fenna, taking a big gulp from her glass. I was out walking in the woods there by myself the other day and

I wondered: Why not just stay? Nobody would know about me, about this person. Down in the valley I heard the rush of cars heading for the Gotthard Tunnel or Biasca. Up there in the forest, the wind swayed the tops of the fir trees back and forth. Birds were singing. I could feel the mossy stones under the soles of my feet.

Sounds nice, said Luc, looking up from the pan, where the omelette was bubbling.

4

It would be another son, Rahel knew at once, as she held a positive pregnancy test in her hands barely a year after Rico. Weeks later, her new gynaecologist told her she was having a girl. Rahel didn't believe him, and decided to have a midwife do the rest of the examinations. No more ultrasounds.

When Leni was born on 19 December, gushing out of her in a torrent of amniotic fluid and into the pre-heated white towel the midwife was holding, she caught a brief flash of female genitalia. So she had given birth to a daughter, then. She felt sick at the idea.

My little hussy, thought Rahel hours later on the maternity ward, the baby wrapped in green against her stomach. She didn't know how to carry the sentence any further than that. There were just those three words, shaped out of play-doh, lumped into a whole in her mind. Again and again, she shook her head and threw a fleeting glance at her child's small, still-wrinkled face. She wasn't capable of unbuttoning her nightdress and offering the girl her breast. Her belly was a hole into which Leni would fall, back into the womb and through that into nothing.

Suddenly, the covers around Rahel's thighs were warm. She fumbled gingerly for the call button at the top of the bed. One minute later, a nurse appeared and Rahel greeted her with the words: Looks like someone left the floodgates open.

As the nurse smiled and busied herself with the sheets, she felt like a schoolchild who'd made a bad joke. She didn't hear the gentle voice say her name twice, and then again, more distinctly.

Please take a moment to wash yourself in the bathroom so I can change the bedding.

Rahel struggled upright, the baby soft and heavy in her arms. The door opened and Boris came in with a paper cup and a broad grin on his lips. As the smell of coffee filled the room, the nurse assured her that incontinence was very common in the days after a birth and no cause for concern. The sanitary pads she put on the bedside table were even thicker than the ones for the usual postpartum discharge, and Rahel didn't like the idea of using them – she had no desire to see the lochia, the bright-red, earth-scented blood.

Without a word, Boris took Leni and placed her softly in the cot. She lay still. Then he led Rahel by the hand into the bathroom, pulled up her nightdress, removed her mesh underwear, rinsed her vulva with lukewarm water from a big plastic bottle, dried her carefully with a towel and replaced her pad. Rahel felt no pain, just the opening-out that her body had gone through. Tonight, she thought, I've been upended.

In the days that followed, the nurses tried to plug the hole in Rahel's belly with breakfast, lunch and dinner. Fruit, little cakes and coffee were served between meals. Rahel lay in bed with her mouth shut.

Her milk didn't come. Rahel couldn't go home like this, said the midwives, and the doctors didn't want to let her go either. She had to be able to feed her daughter.

Again and again, Boris put Leni to Rahel's breast, trying to stimulate the milk, and Rahel screamed in pain: her nipples were two red, open wounds. At last, the first tentative beads of milk worked loose.

Five days after the birth, on Christmas Eve, they finally went home, and the character of the house was altered at a single stroke. Leni bawled through the cracks in the wood from room to room, all the way up to the attic, where Boris still retreated every day to write for an hour or two. But Rico, who had been staying with Boris's parents for a few days, loved his sister fiercely anyway, from the very beginning. He spent his time playing on his bed in the room they all shared with the baby, and kept glancing over whenever Rahel put Leni down to sleep or dozed off herself. When Rahel nursed her, Rico would come over to her bed with his stuffed sheep, snuggle up to Rahel, watch his sister and feed the sheep with an empty bottle. Only on the nights when Boris took Rico up to bed and he screamed that he was a big brother, that he was allowed to stay up later now, did he ask: When is Leni going back?

Rahel, who was lying on the sofa in the living room and heard every word, pulled the woollen blanket up to her ears. One brief question filled her head: Yes, when?

Rahel didn't switch her phone on, but there were still visitors, who announced themselves through Boris: friends, acquaintances, neighbours, relatives. Even Verena dropped by once, but

Rahel scarcely noticed the people gathered around her bed; she didn't even pay any attention to Fenna, who tried to cheer her up with a homemade chicken-and-rice soup. The mood in the bedroom was churchlike, everyone without exception speaking in hushed tones, a service interrupted only by Leni's crying. Rahel was silent and Boris apologised for her, calmly at first, but as time passed he grew weary and eventually bitter.

She's tired, very tired, the birth didn't go entirely smoothly, and then there's the hormones, the getting used to it, it's been hard, a new situation for everybody, but Rico is delighted with his little sister, and yes, he was finding time to work, and thank you for the little dresses, the little books, the biscuits, do come back, we'd love to see you soon.

Rahel touched the girl as little as possible. When she screamed, she put her in the swing seat in the living room, carried her with outstretched arms, as far away from her as she could, to the high chair in the kitchen and the bed in her room. When Rahel wanted to change her nappy, she stood at the changing table perplexed, a wet wipe in her hand, gazing at the baby's soft skin. Like an illusion, thought Rahel. The pale skin changed colour, all at once turning darker and darker, and Rahel bent down close as the scent of sweet almond oil wafted up to her. Holding her nose with one hand, she pinched rolls of Leni's skin and examined its structure with the other. The darkness was gone. After a few seconds a jolt ran through Rahel. Mechanically she opened the full nappy and cleaned the girl.

Once, three weeks after the birth, Boris came into the room as Rahel was standing there in front of Leni. He asked what was taking so long. When Rahel didn't respond, he pushed her aside, dressed Leni and picked her up.

What is wrong with you? asked Boris.

Rahel pointed at the baby and answered quietly but sharply: She's too big.

You're crazy, he said.

Rahel shrugged.

And you don't give a shit about us.

What do you want from me? demanded Boris loudly. I do the shopping. I play with Rico, I cook and tidy around the house while you're holed up in a darkened bedroom. We've had a baby and your only problem is that the baby is too big?

You're just not there, said Rahel.

Open your eyes!

Boris put Leni on the lambskin rug next to the changing table and covered her.

Something's not right with you, he continued as he straightened back up. You're not well.

Again Rahel shrugged.

Go to the doctor, Rahel.

And what am I supposed to do there? Talk?

For example.

So he can prescribe me some miracle cure that keeps a happy mumsy smile permanently plastered across my face?

Then at least fucking talk to me!

Rahel drummed both fists against her forehead.

It won't work.

She drummed harder, a muffled noise that filled the small room.

Everything in here is gone. It's totally empty!

Boris put his arm around Rahel and pulled her close.

Calm down, he said a little more gently.

I just don't know what to do with a girl, said Rahel, sagging. She let Boris take her whole weight and he clung tightly to her body, which was lighter than ever. Looking up into his round face, she saw his hand brush her fringe behind her ears. Then she saw a bright orangey yellow, a large, rotating bowl of rice. People sat around it with stony smirks, reaching constantly into the bowl, throwing grains of rice into the air, at her. She felt them sting her face, but kept her eyes wide open until she realised the grains of rice were miniature faces, faces that looked more and more like herself and then her sister; Fenna sneered, soundlessly at first, then she burst into a loud noise, a mixture of a hen's cackle and a human laugh; the lights went out, all was quiet. Rahel was lying on a soft surface. Someone was gently touching her right big toe. When she opened her eyes and looked at her feet she saw Rico's small face, his hands, which wandered to her knees. He huddled against her legs without a word. They lay still for a while, until Rahel asked: Where is Leni?

She's asleep on the rug, said Boris.

He got up from the end of the bed.

And you should sleep too, he added. You should rest and recover, and come back to real life.

After a long, twelve-hour sleep from which Rahel awoke feeling numb everywhere, she managed with each new movement to break her aversion to Leni. She looked after her daughter, caring for her day and night as she had done with Rico, even if her hands held the girl more clumsily and the motions seemed more mechanical. The singing was gone. No songs appeared in Rahel's mind, not one single melody. Suddenly her milk was flowing in vast quantities. But the milk and the girl didn't slot things into place – far from it. Rahel watched Boris with faint revulsion as he horsed around with the kids, stroking Leni's pale, downy hair, putting his finger in her mouth to suck. She could barely stand to be held by him anymore.

The weeks passed. Leni's mealtimes set the family rhythm: every four hours, feed after feed. No one was surprised when, at three and a half months, she began to refuse the breast. She would lie in Rahel's arms, staring round-eyed in apparent boredom at her already dripping nipple. Rahel pumped milk and kept it in an empty bottle in the fridge. Rico loved his cereal with Mama milk, and for Leni's lunch and dinner Rahel started cooking puréed carrot.

5

Around quarter to nine the telephone rang. Rico let himself slip out of his chair, arms aloft, as though expecting to land on a trampoline. He stayed sitting on the floor and Rahel got to her feet.

Wash your hands, she called to him on the way to the phone, which hung on the wall in the corridor – an old model with a rotary dial that Boris's grandparents had used.

Rahel picked up and gave her name. Fenna was on the other end of the line. Her voice was distorted by a faint crackle, and soft, as though from another world. She was coming round for a visit, she declared, and would ideally travel to Gesswil that day – she could be on the doorstep in three or four hours. Despite the crackle she sounded solemn, which Rahel only wondered about after she'd hung up. Fenna, bringer of good luck from afar, as always.

When she went back into the kitchen Rico's seat was empty, Leni was dozing in her chair and there was no sign of Boris. It wasn't until half past eight that Rahel stood up, holding Leni, and heard Rico coming down the stairs from the attic. When she asked if Boris was in his study, he nodded almost imperceptibly.

You only got together with me because I was the first sucker to come along, Boris had accused her the previous night, once the children were asleep.

And you've come to this conclusion because I insist on sharing our bedroom with the kids? Rahel had said.

You're living off my money in my house with your kids, the way you see fit.

They're our kids, for fuck's sake, they're ours!

I'm not the one making that distinction. You are.

What do you mean by that?

You don't care where I stand in any of this. You won't budge an inch to meet me in the middle. You're shutting me out. More and more.

With that Boris had taken himself up to the attic. Rahel had let her head drop back, and stayed in that position at the kitchen table until she got cold and went to bed.

With a jagged sweep Rahel brushed the crumbs off the table and switched on the vacuum cleaner, which stood handy behind the door. As the hoover droned in her ears and the memory of her fight with Boris was gradually shooed aside, she wondered when she'd last seen her sister apart from at Gesswil. She remembered Fenna's graduation ceremony three years earlier. Rahel had watched her from the gallery, a newly minted primary-school teacher, barely twenty-three, accepting her diploma onstage with glowing cheeks. It wasn't the first time she'd looked at her sister and thought that her father must have been some god from Norse mythology, a man like Thor.

Years ago Verena had had a postcard of the god of thunder, which she left on the coffee table for months. He was depicted as a blond youth standing upright in a chariot, his strapping body clad in tight-fitting red robes and his left hand clutching the head of a fallen man by the hair. The man was staring wide-eyed at the thorns tied to the chariot, while in his right hand Thor held a hammer, ready to strike.

The sight of all this brimming masculinity had sent a quiver through Rahel, leaving a warmth in the pit of her stomach that seeped over the next few days into every cell in her body. Fenna's thirst for freedom had to be genetic, Rahel was convinced, passed down from a man like that Thor.

Fenna had brought a big leather bag, but dropped its handle the moment Rahel opened the door. Rahel squinted in the noonday sun, and for a few seconds the figure opposite was only a dark, sharply silhouetted plane. By the time she could see clearly again, her sister was leaning in and hugging her. A warm, throbbing body. After a moment they broke apart, Fenna wiping beads of sweat from her upper lip with the back of her hand.

I remembered the walk to your place being a bit shorter, she said.

Well, you're here now, said Rahel.

I'm so glad. I'll stay the night, if I may. Or possibly longer.

She gave Rahel a questioning look.

Assuming you can put me up, she added.

Rahel gestured inside the house.

Why don't you come in first?

Boris, who had emerged from his study just before lunch, came into the hall and greeted Fenna with three kisses on the cheek. Behind him stood Rico, who held out a toy car to Fenna, beaming. His fine hair was light against his head, bouncing every time he moved.

He still had one or two things to be getting on with, said Boris, but he'd have more time later. Blowing Rico a kiss and nodding at Rahel, he crunched away across the gravel drive towards his car. Rahel, Fenna and Rico watched as he started the engine and drove off.

Is he in a rush? asked Fenna.

Apparently, said Rahel, closing the front door. Then she added: You can stay as long as that works for everybody.

Fenna took off her shoes and followed Rahel and Rico into the living room. Leni, who had been snoozing on a playmat next to the TV, woke with a start and immediately began to cry. Rahel picked her up.

Ah, there's the little mouse! She's grown! Fenna said.

Rahel put the baby in her arms.

Would you like something to eat? she asked.

Thanks, I've already had something.

Fancy a coffee?

Fenna nodded.

She sat down with Leni at the kitchen table, holding her firmly in her lap with both hands. Leni peered around curiously while Rahel poured ground coffee into the moka pot and set it on the hob. Rico came into the kitchen too, pulled his chair out almost inaudibly and sat up at the table. Fenna asked him how he liked the nice house and his little sister. Rico answered in monosyllables: yes, no, Leni, games.

The coffee pot bubbled. Rahel poured two mugs and handed one to Fenna.

Alright, said Rahel. Why are you here?

Am I in the way?

Not at all.

I'm always amazed at how remote this place is.

Rahel sat down opposite Fenna and cupped the mug in her hands.

I feel like I'm always stuck at home. At first I thought it had felt that way since Leni was born, but actually it's been the same ever since I moved in.

Fenna stroked Leni's head twice, then let her hand drop and said: How about a silly night? I'm sure that'd cheer you up.

Guzzling eggs, Verena-style? replied Rahel. No thanks.

We can celebrate in our own way.

And invite Inge?

Haha.

And get some of Boris's clothes so we look as Verena-ishly masculine as possible, right?

What's the matter with you? asked Fenna.

Don't talk to me about silly nights. That's the last thing I need. Or let's put it this way: it's just silly.

Fenna shook her head slightly back and forth. Don't you remember how Verena explained it? Silly comes from the Old High German *salig*, happy, and yeah, actually I'd quite like to have a nice happy evening, maybe get a bit merry.

Let's change the subject, Rahel said, putting her mug down with a jerk.

Fenna gazed for a few seconds through the kitchen window, looking at the apple tree outside. Then she turned back to Rahel and asked: Why didn't you come and see me last time you were in Zurich?

I had things to do, said Rahel promptly.

I'd have liked to offer you a drink.

Rahel picked at the skin around her thumbnail with her middle finger.

God knows where Boris has got to, she said.

Let me guess: the pub or the library.

A flake of skin came off and Rahel rolled it between her fingers into a tiny ball.

He makes himself scarce more and more these days, she said.

Tough time?

When Rahel didn't answer, Fenna slipped a thumb under her bra strap and let it snap back against her skin.

You're all glued together in this little house like those happy family paper cut-outs. You need fresh air!

Are you still working at the same café?

At Gerald's. I quit the day before yesterday.

Really?

Yeah. They let me leave without a notice period. So I'm not there anymore.

Are you happy?

What do you mean?

You seem different somehow, Rahel said. Depleted. Luc?

Everything's fine with Luc, so far.

Rico stood up. Are you coming to play? he asked Fenna.

She promised him she'd play later and turned Leni – who had started to whimper – to face her. They sat belly to belly, the little girl clutching Fenna's curly hair in her small hands.

Time for your lunch break, Rahel told Rico. You can go play for a while in your room.

Rico ducked his head and left the kitchen as quietly as he had entered it.

Thirsty? Fenna pointed at Leni.

We've just eaten, answered Rahel. She walked around the table and picked up her daughter.

She reminds me of you sometimes, she went on, looking first at Fenna, then at Leni. Rahel sat down with the baby. A little ball of energy, just like you.

Is that a compliment?

A fact. You both do what you want.

And you don't?

Rahel clasped her daughter a little tighter in her lap.

OK, tell me. Is Luc giving you a hard time?

Hesitantly, Fenna shook her head. That's not it. I'm pregnant.

Aha, said Rahel, almost tonelessly, leaning back. Leni lay against her upper body as though on a deckchair.

Do you have any idea what you're letting yourself in for? she asked. No more cigarettes. No booze. No wonder you look depleted.

Anything else you might be missing?

Look at me! This is what kids do to you.

Rahel pointed to a whitish fleck of vomit on her shirt.

Your pessimism makes me sick too.

And what does Luc think?

Touchy subject, said Fenna.

I thought so. Luc, a dad.

We don't need a dad.

Fenna reached for the sugar bowl, which was next to a stack of post at the edge of the table, and heaped two spoonfuls into her coffee.

I haven't taken a test, and he can't deal with that.

What do you mean, a test? asked Rahel.

I missed my period and the signs have been obvious, said Fenna.

Are you broke or something?

Sorry?

You know you can go into literally any supermarket and buy a pregnancy test for a couple of francs?

That's not the issue.

Fenna, did you really come here, of all places, to look for advice? asked Rahel. It's a bit late for that, surely?

OK, fine, I needed some space from Luc, Fenna said. And he needs time to come to his senses. Plus I wanted to see you. I was hoping some of your levelheadedness would rub off, but clearly you've managed to lose that somewhere along the line.

Is it just about the test or is it the pregnancy that's bothering Luc? Rahel asked.

I don't know. Nor does he.

Sounds like you've got yourself into a pickle.

Yeah, yeah.

Rahel reached one arm across Leni's small body and lifted her mug to her lips with her free hand. She was trembling a little, and swiftly put the mug back down.

Do you ever think about our dad? she asked.

Why should I?

Ever since Leni was born he keeps popping into my head. No idea why, but maybe we should face up to all that stuff properly one of these days. To him walking out.

You already have – in your songs, said Fenna. I don't need anything like that, and our so-called dad has absolutely nothing to do with Luc.

You sure?

Anyway, what about Martin? asked Fenna, instead of replying. Lowering her voice, she continued after a short pause: Have you ever got the sense Rico is missing him?

Rico doesn't know that Boris isn't his biological father. But we were talking about something else.

Rico has you and Boris. He's fine. Why would he need Martin? He was conceived by him – yay, biology – and that's that. I don't need my dad any more than Rico needs his.

And that's why you don't need a father for your child? asked Rahel.

You don't know anything about what's going on between Luc and me.

Then tell me.

Fenna got to her feet.

Not now. I've got a splitting headache. I'd like to go and lie down for a bit.

All I want is to know you're OK, said Rahel.

Let me worry about that.

Fenna smiled, but it didn't reach her eyes.

You've changed so much, Rahel said.

You're one to talk.

The two fell silent for a moment.

Will you tell me more about it later? asked Rahel.

Mmm.

Fenna stood in the doorway, holding the mug of coffee in one hand and her bag in the other.

Leni and I will come upstairs with you and show you your room, said Rahel.

6

Egg binge, Fenna had always replied, when Luc asked her in those first few weeks what she wanted him to cook. She had loved sitting at the kitchen table, watching him: the way he rolled up his sleeves and set out all the ingredients on the table, the way his brow furrowed as he cracked the eggs on the rim of the pan, the way he gave her a brief squeeze as he walked past.

Ever since she was a child, eggs had been special to Fenna. Verena had only served them on her silly nights, in every possible variation: fried or poached, scrambled, in French or Spanish omelettes, hard boiled on a bed of salad or in mustard sauce. She would hold the eggs in her hands for ages before preparing them. Over and over she told Fenna and Rahel how an egg was formed, how hens had one sole ovary and one sole fallopian tube, and how ovulation was a daily thing for them, except when they were brooding. Verena's voice had been soft as she explained that the chicken stored the rooster's sperm inside her body. It could be two weeks from mating to fertilisation, because the chicken only released the sperm once the egg was ready.

Fenna used to gobble down the eggs on silly nights. Early on she'd realised those evenings were only possible because they were a household of women, to which Inge also belonged. The father Rahel sometimes talked about didn't interest Fenna much. Not then, and not now. Only for a phase during puberty had Fenna been disgusted by the hen's eggs: by the yellow ball of yolk that formed in the hen's ovary and made its long way down the fallopian tube to be fertilised; by the white, which was produced by little glands and cocooned the yolk. It seemed perverse to Fenna that three days after an egg was laid you could actually see the chick's heartbeat through the shell, unless it was taken away from the chicken. Verena relished every egg she ate. A high-performing hen laid three hundred eggs per year, while one in the wild laid fifty; there were fifty-two weeks in a year, and she, Verena, ate an egg every two weeks, half what a hen laid in nature. She thought that was justifiable, she said when Fenna confronted her.

The chicken feeds me and I honour the chicken.

Fenna made friends with eggs again relatively quickly after her period of aversion. She still thought there was something questionable about the number of eggs Verena consumed, and she said so every time they went out to feast. Verena was rigorous about not buying any food that contained fresh or powdered eggs, but away from home she ate anything, and after every restaurant meal she treated herself to a small glass of advocaat. When she moved out, Fenna left Verena's thing about eggs behind. In her own household she paid no attention to ingredients. She ate what she wanted, and eggs were definitely on the list.

Fenna was astonished to realise years later that her sister was fond of eggs too, because on silly nights Rahel had rarely finished her plate. Eggs had been the main component of Rahel's wedding dinner. That afternoon, after the civil ceremony, she had conjured eight of them out of the fridge. Since only the two witnesses present at their vows – apart from three-month-old Rico – were invited to the meal afterwards at Rahel and Boris's, eight had been enough. Rahel had served *spicy eggs in a nest* – fried eggs with stir-fried vegetables – as a starter, while the main course was scrambled eggs with mushrooms and narrow strips of wholemeal toast. Fenna had taken small bites and chewed slowly, knowing she wouldn't start feeling full for at least twenty minutes. As Boris drove her to the station afterwards, however, she felt her appetite roar back, and although she'd sworn to go straight to the platform and wait for the Zurich train, she made a beeline for the station café and bought a large tuna sandwich. As she ate the soggy bread, she suddenly realised how happy she was to have been part of the wedding party, even though she herself didn't see the point of marriage and had no intention of marrying. She loved too much and too wildly. Swallowing a half-chewed bite, Fenna grinned at the memory of the couple at the registry office. Rahel had stood straight as a poker, with her ear-length brown hair – she cut it herself in front of the bathroom mirror, so it tended to be a bit uneven – falling over the right half of her face. She had leant towards Boris and said something Fenna didn't catch from a distance. Then she turned away from him again, her jaw clenched. The blazer, which made her shoulders much too wide, emphasised her lean frame. Boris, with his full cheeks, one hand in his trouser pocket and the other on the handlebar of the buggy, had seemed relaxed, peering into it with a smile.

An odd couple, Fenna had thought, and a nice one. If her sister was going to pair up with someone long-term, it would have to be a big bear of a man like Boris, not mummy's boy Chris with his cute little ears or that freak Martin. She wasn't surprised that Rahel had married Boris after such a short time. From the off, Rahel was just as direct and opened up just as quickly as she did. If you're going to get married, then do it now, thought Fenna.

Not long after the wedding, Fenna finished her teacher's training and took a full-time job at a school in the city. It was a shock, finding herself back in the working world, which proved tougher than she'd imagined. More and more she spent the weekends at home, not at bars with friends or by the lake, as she had done in the past. After a week of school she was too busy recharging her batteries and getting her bearings, as she put it: doing laundry, cooking for herself, reading a lot. I'm turning into a couch potato, she thought each morning, as she inspected her rear end in the tall mirror. It had been looking wobbly lately and was getting wider every day, while the students got slower by the week at finishing her assignments. Before long they were lagging behind the syllabus. When, towards the end of the second quarter, Fenna tore up one of her Year Four students' exercise sheets into sixteen pieces in front of the whole class, hands shaking with rage, she realised her impatience had got the better of her. Already. The class laughed as she let the shreds of paper sail to the floor, and Fenna took their laughter with her arms hanging by her sides.

Chop chop, sit down everyone, she shouted.

Only the boy whose exercise sheet she'd torn up remained standing, his face stony.

Fenna grabbed him by the shoulder, but he shook off her hand and flopped down onto the ground with his arms crossed.

She decided at that moment that her career as a primary-school teacher was over, at least for the next couple of years. That same evening, she gave notice that she was quitting at the end of the school year.

In the remaining months she tried to reorient herself, mulling over potential training courses and further education, going to lectures on all sorts of topics and starting to socialise more frequently again. One of the lectures she attended was on Syria. Fenna had hoped to learn more about the country's history as well as new approaches to the current situation, but what she got was a monologue from a sixty-year-old man who described himself as a globetrotter and talked exclusively about himself. His exotic trip had been fifteen years ago. Apart from Fenna, Luc was the only one who left the anecdote-peppered lecture before the end. He was fearless enough to brave the disapproving stares from countless members of the audience, who were listening to the old man like worshippers in church; a few seconds later, Fenna followed his example. In the foyer they walked past the canapés already laid out on buffet tables and stepped outside, Fenna behind Luc. He spun ninety degrees, eyed Fenna for a brief moment then took a step towards her.

Gross, said Luc.

She lit a cigarette.

The canapés? she asked.

That guy.

Fenna laughed and surveyed him. He was wearing shorts that revealed muscular calves, and was shifting foot to foot, as though on the verge of sprinting away. His face was lined, but he couldn't be much older than thirty, she thought.

Are you going to the dance show they mentioned?

Luc shook his head.

It was a massive let-down coming at all. I had the wrong idea about the event.

Fenna looked at the busy road lined by five tall saplings. The sky was cloudless.

Have you ever been to the Middle East? she asked.

Luc said he hadn't.

I do travel to India and Nepal quite a lot. How about you?

No big trips, she said. My name's Fenna, by the way.

Luc, he said, tapping his chest with the flat of his hand.

And what takes you to India?

Trekking. The mountains there are incredible.

You don't have to travel that far to go hiking, said Fenna.

That's where you're wrong, he retorted. The Himalayas are massive. Infinitely vast. You can't compare them to the mountains in Switzerland.

I only know them from pictures.

Luc shifted his weight from one foot to the other.

Up there in the Himalayas, it's like a kind of meditation, he said.

He looked Fenna in the eye. He radiated warmth; there was a lightness about him, something obliging, yet at the same time Fenna sensed this was hiding something else, something dark she wanted to see.

I bet you could find that in Switzerland too, she said, stubbing out her cigarette on the ground.

Voices could be heard inside the building. Two women wandered out onto the pavement, one of them cramming puff pastry into her mouth. Luc and Fenna looked at one another and laughed.

Fancy a walk? We could head towards Sihlwald, she said.

That'll take at least four hours.

Fenna nodded.

OK, said Luc. I'm headed in that direction anyway.

Together they walked down the street, Luc next to Fenna. His movements were lithe and agile, his pace matched hers. The asphalt was saturated with sunlight that afternoon, and Fenna felt as though she was walking through a gigantic sauna. She kept scrutinising Luc's face, his chest, his legs; she would have liked to press herself against him, her sweat running down his smooth skin, drop by drop.

They lost track of the most direct way to Sihlwald. Instead they meandered through the streets, eventually sitting down at a café and ordering martinis on the rocks.

After a while Luc said he was going home. She could come with him, if she liked. He lived nearby with a couple of colleagues.

Sure, I can come.

You want to?

Yeah.

In his room Luc opened the window, stood in front of it, and turned to Fenna. She went up to him until they were chest to chest, stomach to stomach, knee to knee, and she kissed him, slowly at first, gently, then ran her tongue over his lips and slipped it into his mouth. In the past, in situations like these, Fenna had always dragged whoever she was with straight into bed; she had undressed, still standing, taken their hands and laid them on her breasts, her bottom, her belly; you can do anything to me, she had whispered, but inevitably, before long she would refuse to use her tongue when she kissed them – too slippery or too dry, too hasty or too wet. With Luc, everything was different. Kissing him by the window was enough for her that first night. She wished she could store her arousal in her whole body, so that afterwards she could press the repeat button, like on a CD player, and listen to the same song over and over again. When eventually she left the flat with a piece of Luc's raw-food apple pie in her belly, she felt sated.

A pitta recipe, Luc had said, chewing, as they sat at the tobacco- and breadcrumb-strewn kitchen table.

What do you mean, pitta? Is it cake or bread? asked Fenna.

I mean the dosha. Pitta.

Dosha?

The pitta life force. It comes from Ayurveda.

Well, it's delicious, anyway.

Pitta is my dosha, Luc went on. This is a recipe for pitta people.

Hmm, said Fenna.

Pittas tend towards hyperacidity. Raw food is perfect for me. And it's bound to be good for you too, as a kapha type, he said. Fresh fruit, raw vegetables and small, light meals will do you good. And you'd better lay off the cigarettes, too.

Fenna laughed. You're getting a bit ahead of yourself.

Want any more? he asked.

Fenna pointed at her stomach. Full for today, she said, and a few minutes later she was setting off. She was determined not to contact Luc before the three-day period she had set herself was up. Back home, however, she couldn't help herself, and sent him a WhatsApp.

Will you cook kapha for me sometime?

The next morning she still hadn't received a response, nor by midday. That evening he texted. Sure, he said, he could do next week or the week after that, if she wanted. He had a great cookbook.

Kapha, googled Fenna, and came across a site that said people with the kapha dosha were associated with qualities like heaviness, fatness and cold, which made this type resistant to influence; lethargy and obesity would dog her all her life. Fenna swallowed hard. The thought of their kiss suddenly made her feel hot. Shame and arousal sat cheek by jowl, and she slammed her fist angrily on the table. She wanted Luc, and she wanted him now.

Today or tomorrow, she texted.

Just did a shop. You coming? was the response, half an hour later.

Already on my way, she wrote.

Eventually Luc served tofu schnitzel and oven chips, saying he'd made a mistake: she wasn't kapha after all, she was vata-kapha, and he hadn't been able to find a recipe for vata-kaphas at short notice. What he had here was completely neutral.

She laughed.

I like you, he said, giving her a long hug after she'd swallowed the last bite and washed it down with sweet white wine.

Luc was the first man who hadn't immediately capitulated to Fenna, playing with her instead. Playing along. But although things initially progressed at breakneck speed, months later Fenna still knew virtually nothing about him, even though they met once or twice a week when he was in Switzerland. After graduating from school, Luc had started three different courses, dropping out each time after a few semesters. Since then he'd been working temp jobs, all short-term and mainly in IT. He travelled to Asia as often as he could, partly to hike but also for yoga and meditation classes.

Luc filled her flat with a new scent, her mind with ideas, and, above all, her body with life. Since Fenna had started working at a café in the old town she was tired in the evenings again, but it was different from when she'd been a teacher. She was out a lot, drifting from one bar to the next, with friends and with Luc. Fenna liked the city, but she preferred the outdoors. Sometimes she and Luc went hiking together. The Bosco d'Öss, a forest in Ticino, was still on their imaginary to-do list. So was the Jura. And Fenna was still dreaming of a farm, of her own chickens and eggs. Of breathing life into something she had chosen for herself.

Five months after she met Luc, he mentioned during the interval at the cinema that he occasionally saw other women. Fenna dropped back into the thickly padded seat him as he drummed his index fingers on the backrest in front of him.

I never thought of what's going on between us as a relationship, he said, and his fingers stopped drumming as he fixed his dark eyes on her.

At that moment the lights went out and the film started up again. Fenna turned to face the screen, where a woman in a car was leaning back as she held the wheel, dark sunglasses on her face and blonde hair in the wind. *I'm so much happier now that I'm dead*, she said.

Fenna grabbed Luc's hand and stood up. Together they left the cinema, Luc following.

Outside she wanted to know what was going on between him and the other women. Luc was quiet for a while.

It's just about sex.

Am I not enough for you?

It's nothing to do with that. It's just what I need, that's all. Different bodies.

So much for being a vegetarian, hissed Fenna.

You know exactly what I mean, Luc said, roughly grabbing hold of her upper arm.

Fenna tore herself away.

And how do you think you're going to keep bodies and emotions separate? she asked.

When Luc didn't answer, Fenna gave him an ultimatum: her and only her, or nothing.

He would think about it, Luc said coolly.

We're still in a relationship even now, she added. Even now, Luc.

Then she turned on her heel and went.

You don't need him but you still want him, she said to herself in a low voice as she flung her bag on the floor and tugged off her clothes. She got into bed naked, took out her phone and considered calling Verena. She'd get no advice from her mother, not about men – she never had. Fenna could hear her mother's answer now: For me it was the other way around. I didn't want him but I still needed him, your father.

Three weeks later, a postcard from Kathmandu fluttered into her letterbox. He had made up his mind, wrote Luc in his usual scrawl. He was ready for her now. It wasn't much of a surprise. Fenna had been sure it was only a matter of time before he came knocking again, and she rubbed her hands. Folding the postcard into a small rectangle, she tucked it into her wallet like a trophy. She thought about it often as she walked through town, her bag slung over her right shoulder.

When he got back they agreed to commit to a monogamous relationship. Fenna suspected that Luc didn't keep his promise, that he slept with other women, at least when he was travelling. She, too, began to see other men from time to time, and women, like before. These flings didn't mean much to her: the orgasms were slightly stronger than when she masturbated, but never as intense as with Luc. He'd be glad she had a good time while he was gone, she told herself.

7

They went into the guest bedroom, and suddenly, as Rahel stood beside the big bed with Leni in her arms, she felt like sinking into it with her sister. She wanted to soak into the sheets like melted resin, and she wanted to remember – hundreds, thousands of years back, to a warm dark place where time elapsed without being counted, where bodies grew, brought forth new bodies, then passed into the earth, into the grass.

I'll just rest here with you a minute, OK? asked Rahel.

Of course.

Fenna pulled back the duvet.

Rahel placed Leni in the middle of the mattress and lay down next to her. Fenna took a thin pullover from her bag, put it on and stretched out on the bed as well.

Feel this, she said, pulling up her top, taking Rahel's hand and positioning it on her stomach.

A regular pulse behind the abdominal wall. Leni, between the two sisters, was breathing calmly. The girl had closed her eyes. The lids looked like they'd been drawn on with a sharp pencil; her cheeks glinted. Rahel, too, shut her eyes, giving herself over to the darkness, slipping into a doze. She saw skin, a landscape on which a shadow was cast. The shadow wandered, refashioning the skin first this way, then that: in some places a glossy, gleaming surface, in others rough and cratered terrain.

Everywhere, fine antennae-like hairs unbent out of scarcely visible openings in the skin, conducting sensations from place to place in twitching bolts of lightning; they bored into the skin, beneath the flesh, beneath the layer of fat; and in the womb, hidden, was a child shifting to and fro, putting its thumb in its mouth. Rahel sighed and Fenna's belly tensed under her hand.

8

Fenna and Luc didn't get to the Bosco d'Öss – the wild woods, as she had pitched them – until a year after they first met. They started their hike in Airolo and climbed the sunny side of the Valle Leventina; to the right, the valley ran parallel to the ridgeway. The murmur of cars heading north to south or south to north along the motorway kept drifting towards them. To the left, they could have climbed even further: Pizzo Taneda, Pizzo del Sole, Pizzo di Campello. Fenna looked around, gazing towards the forests that stretched dark and elegant from the valley towards the mountain peaks, and above them the summits. They passed stretches of meadow and forest, walked by countless stone dwellings. The houses seemed somehow primeval, as though formed not by humans but by nature. Some were still inhabited, others derelict; roofs were missing or had fallen in. Sometimes only vestiges of wall remained, grass growing in the cracked stone. Fenna's legs moved as if of their own accord – she felt light this morning. Luc answered her questions reluctantly. He'd slept badly, he said, and yes, of course he was enjoying the sun, and no, he couldn't imagine the animals and smugglers that had once trudged along this path, the trains of mules and packhorses.

Pausing outside a deserted stone cabin on the mountainside, Fenna said that this, this part of Switzerland, was the kind of gap she had been talking about. She animated them as she walked through them. A gap in which she was suspended.

Without replying, Luc strode on.

After just over three hours they reached the Bosco d'Öss. Here, at the highest point, the trail bent and led into the forest, which was on a slope. At last the trees swallowed the sound of the cars.

It's all more beautiful than I'd thought, said Luc.

Dumping his rucksack on the ground, he took out a bottle of water. Fenna put her hands on her hips.

So, here's the Swiss wilderness for you, she said.

Luc held out the bottle to her. Want some?

Fenna took a few sips and handed it back to Luc.

Öss. Makes me think of Ötzi, she said. It's the kind of place where you end up getting found in thousands of years, still in your hiking boots.

Naked? asked Luc.

Naked, said Fenna. Leathery skin, reddish and discoloured, a man and a woman, and they'll wonder: Which was which?

Fenna put her hands on Luc's shoulders and pulled him close. She unzipped his jacket centimetre by centimetre, as though unwrapping a long-anticipated gift. Then she slipped her hand into the neck of his jumper and looked up at him aslant, her eyes slightly narrowed.

Forget it, said Luc, gripping her hand. You can still tell the difference from the pelvic bones, even thousands of years on.

Luc grabbed Fenna around the hips and patted her bottom.

I'd have to be blind not to realise you're a woman, he said. And deaf.

Fenna broke away and took a step back.

Tell me if I'm getting on your nerves, she said.

Well, that's women for you.

You and your bullshit stereotypes.

Not stereotypes. Biology!

Again, Luc lunged for Fenna's hips.

Come on, he said. What was all that stuff about the man and woman up here? Animating the gap?

Fenna pushed Luc's hands away again, taking a step backwards.

Screw you, she said sharply.

Luc came right up to Fenna; she felt his breath on her face as he stared long into her eyes. He kissed her roughly on the lips. She tried to turn away, but he was gripping her head tightly. With all her strength she grabbed his forearms, yanked them aside and bit down. His cheeks felt astonishingly soft in her mouth, the stubble chafing her tongue. She pulled away and shoved him in the chest, laughing.

Fine, he said in a jerky voice.

Again he grabbed her. Fenna stumbled. He wrapped his arm around her upper body and dragged her deeper into the woods. She screamed; thorns gouged at her legs. After a few metres Luc stopped beside a large root protruding from the earth, and in one swift movement he pulled down her trousers, held up only by a loose elastic waistband. He pulled down her knickers too. Turning her, he tipped her upper body forward as though she were made of rubber. Luc thrust into her from behind. One hand clenched in the earth, she tried uselessly to loosen his grip with the other. Each jolt brought her face closer to the ground, until her left cheek touched the soil. Luc gave a shrill, short cry. Then he broke away from her. He dropped down next to Fenna, who lay quivering on the ground. They lay for minutes, back to back. She heard birds and the distant drone of a plane; she stared into the springtime colours of the forest, the lush pale green of the mosses and ferns, the dark green of the pines. It burned between her legs. After what seemed like an age, she felt Luc's hand on her stomach. With the other he pulled up her knickers and trousers, which had slipped to her ankles. Fenna got slowly to her feet. Scooping up a handful of earth, she flung it into his face.

What? he asked.

She shook her head and trudged back down the trail, where she picked up her rucksack and kept walking steeply downhill. Quick steps. Over and over, her whole body shook. The woods thinned out and she reached a hill. For a moment, Fenna stopped and stared, gazing out across the Valle Leventina and the snow-capped mountains beyond. Then she walked unhurriedly towards the valley, maintaining a steady pace. She heard Luc's steps behind her. He called her name several times. After the fifth time, she swung around.

Piss off, she screamed.

Luc was pale, his face somehow fogged. As though he hadn't heard her, he walked on in silence after her.

It was more than an hour's climb back down to Osco, where traders had once rested with their animals. Fenna sat down on a bench outside the church. Luc flopped down in the meadow three metres away. She opened her rucksack and began to eat the food they'd brought: Luc's sandwich and hers, the half-pack of dried fruit, the rest of the biscuits, his iced tea, her orange juice. She emptied her water bottle down to the last drop and finally felt herself close up inside, felt a line now drawn between them, between Luc and herself. She tried to burp, but she was so full that no air came out.

Our bus leaves in ten minutes, she said, shouldering her rucksack.

They took a small postbus to Faido then switched to the train. Fenna didn't say a word the entire journey. Luc sat cross-legged next to her, staring into space. Their carriage was packed with tourists who, like them, had spent the Easter weekend in Ticino. Fenna felt sick. She gazed out of the window into the valley, as they left metre after metre of elevation behind them. After Airolo they were swallowed by the darkness. As they rushed through the Gotthard Tunnel, the train car distended in the belly of the mountain, the people were mirrored in the windows either side, and the carriage grew wider and wider. Then an old, new world opened up: Göschenen, wooded scenery, rivers, more tiny villages. Eventually they reached Lake Lucerne.

Not until they disembarked at Zurich and Fenna set off towards the main concourse did Luc grab her arm again.

What now? he asked.

You wanker, said Fenna hoarsely. How dare you.

You wanted it too.

What? I wanted you to drag me off? Rape me?

Luc took a step back.

Wow, he said. That's how you look at it?

Did you see me joining in?

I didn't see you struggling.

Fenna slapped Luc in the face. Turning on her heel, she marched briskly towards the escalator that led down to the underground tracks. A film was unspooling in her head – dark, bleary pictures of that April day. Pictures that were still there when she got home, stood under the shower for a long time and finally went to bed.

I'm sorry, Luc texted three times. Fenna was abruptly wide awake. Deep down she was ashamed, she realised now. Ashamed of giving Luc the silent treatment for so long and for slapping his face. Because, when all was said and done, it was true: she hadn't really struggled. Once more she rewound the film in her head, back to the moment when Luc had grabbed her, and she wasn't sure now if she'd screamed in fear or pleasure. What mattered was that she hadn't struggled enough, and in the end she'd let him do it, thought Fenna. Something in her must have wanted it, or she wouldn't have provoked him. She shut her eyes.

In the days that followed, Luc's sharp contours smeared. Fenna didn't contact him. In the mornings she sat by the window for hours, gazing at the three fig trees soaking up the sunlight on her neighbour's balcony. She was cold. Yet she felt stronger by the minute. The more time passed, the newer and more tangible her image of Luc became, and above all her image of herself. In the Bosco d'Öss, all Luc had done was reveal his dark side more clearly than ever: the side that had flared up again and again in the course of their relationship, frightening and fascinating her in equal measure.

On the fourth day Fenna dialled Rahel's number. Pressed the red button. Then she tapped in Verena's number. Pressed the red button. They wouldn't understand. Fenna still fundamentally rejected what Luc had said about the differences between men and women. He didn't get the distinction between biology and socialisation. Still, she did now concede something she would never have dared think before: could she have experienced that kind of violence with a woman? Fenna called to mind her female colleagues, friends, lovers – and thought not. Luc couldn't help his outburst. It had been the man in him, whether biologically determined or learned through socialisation. Regardless, it was the maleness she'd been wanting to see ever since she met him. She had opened up to Luc too much, wished too long for him to breathe yet more life into her body and its expanses, she knew that now. She had to completely reshape her relationship with him.

After ignoring for more than a week his pleas to see her, she bought a bottle of Prosecco at the wine shop and invited him over. She was waiting at the kitchen table with two empty crystal glasses.

I forgive you, Fenna declared, while Luc was still standing in the hall.

She opened the bottle. The cork smacked into the ceiling, and Fenna added: But you still owe me.

I didn't mean to hurt you, Luc said.

Fenna handed him a glass, foam spilling over the rim.

I don't want to hear any more about it, she said.

Luc stared at her in amazement.

It was what it was, she added. I can live with it.

A couple of months after the incident in the Bosco d'Öss, she threw her half-finished box of pills in the bin. For way too many years she'd been pumping her body full of artificial hormones. From now on, she informed Luc, they'd be using the temperature method as protection. She wrote out schedules so he could see which evenings he was allowed to come over, what they would do and whether he was permitted to spend the night. They were on their way to a mature relationship, she thought. Sometimes it shrank to a couple of meet-ups per month, then it would swell back up, grow more intense, their encounters more frequent, their activities more diverse. When Luc stayed the night, she usually woke up long before him, warmed a cup of milk and honey in the kitchen and smoked her early morning cigarette.

On one such morning, with the sweet, heavy taste of milk in her mouth and while Luc was still asleep, she realised she was pregnant. Her period was weeks late. Suddenly, the faint tug in her lower abdomen and the pinch in her nipples made sense.

Slowly, she stubbed out her half-smoked cigarette in the ashtray with the tiny crown engraved under every indentation. She got up and emptied it in the bin, put a drop of detergent on the dry sponge, turned on the tap and cleaned it. Fenna had bought it three years earlier, the day she moved out of Verena's place, to christen her flat with a touch of ceremony. She dried it with a tea towel and was putting it in the cupboard behind the shot glasses when there was a sudden pain in her chest. Fenna made a guttural noise. She gripped the sink with both hands, tears dripping onto her dressing gown. Then she felt two hands clasp her waist.

I'm pregnant, Fenna said calmly.

She turned to Luc and kissed him on the right cheek; he smelled of sleep.

Did you just take a test? he asked, in a faintly husky voice.

I don't have to.

Your period's a few days late again and suddenly you think you're pregnant?

Fenna stared angrily at Luc.

Can you think of another explanation? You're such a meditation snob – you can listen to your body, but I'm supposed to test mine?

Luc rubbed his still-drowsy eyes with the back of his hand.

We need to be sure, he said.

Why? If the baby's there, it will grow. I'll feel it, and you'll see it.

That'll take way too long.

Do you not want me to have this baby?

Luc let his arms drop, pushed her aside, turned on the tap and took three huge gulps.

Hello, I'm talking to you, said Fenna.

He straightened back up.

It's quarter past six in the morning, he said. And you're talking about a baby I'm supposed to be happy about, even though it doesn't say anywhere that we're actually expecting it.

You don't trust me, Fenna said.

Luc turned around and left the kitchen. Fenna followed.

Look at me, she said loudly.

Luc was rummaging in his shoulder bag, which lay next to the bed.

Look at me and tell me I'm not good enough.

It's not about that.

What, then?

It's about knowing if you really are, he said.

If I'm the one woman good enough to have your baby.

If you're really pregnant.

I am.

Take the test.

I don't have one. I don't need one. Or you.

Fenna dropped onto the bed.

Come on, Fenna, let's not have the three-act performance.

Go! said Fenna forcefully. I need time.

Luc took fresh underwear out of his bag and grabbed the clothes draped over the office chair.

I'll just jump in the shower.

You can do that at your place. Get out of my flat!

9

Rahel divided up the rooms of the house where she would like to live alone: one for her good days, one for her bad; a room she only entered when she was ill and one where she only spent time when things were going very well. She would decorate the rooms in different ways: one without windows, wallpapered bright red, another exclusively in glass, with a view of trees; one upholstered with oversized cushions, another furnished with a ceiling-height fridge, chock-full of ripe fruit.

Rahel opened her eyes. Leni and Fenna were lying on the bed in front of her. The door was shut, and there was no sound in the room besides the faint hum of insects outside and the baby's deep and regular breaths.

10

Fenna was standing in his room two days after she'd noticed she was pregnant, her back ramrod straight. Luc sat on the bed in front of her, joggling his left and right heels off the floor in turn as she said:

I'm not taking a test. I'm not testing my body with that plastic shit. I'm not testing this baby, which I want. It will show itself to me, and to you, whether you want it to or not. You're going to be a dad.

She paused, fixed her eyes on his feet and continued. I'm going away, maybe for a week or two. Maybe longer. Don't text or call unless you're ready to go down this road with me. If you are, I'll WhatsApp you the address where I'm staying. If I don't hear from you, I'll come back and we'll discuss the rest.

Fenna took a step towards Luc and stood silently before him.

You're not serious! he said.

Deadly serious.

You haven't forgiven me. For what happened up there. In the forest.

Did you actually enjoy it? asked Fenna.

Something came over me.

And you gave in to it.

That wasn't really me.

Yes it was, Fenna said.

I'm sorry.

I've got to go, Luc.

I'll call you, I'll definitely call you, he said.

For a brief moment on the train between Zurich and Gesswil, Fenna didn't know anymore why she'd courted this pregnancy. She felt queasy at the thought of the little heart inside her. How was she supposed to protect it? She looked outside, watching the countryside go by: villages, forests, a garish yellow field of rapeseed, a farmhouse up against the tracks. In the next set of seats, a mother held her two- or three-year-old in her lap. The toddler was sucking on an already-browning piece of apple.

Chocolate, she said to her mother, softly but to Fenna quite audibly, as the woman ruffled her daughter's hair with her hand.

I want chocolate, said the toddler again, louder this time. She looked around. Nobody except for Fenna was paying any attention to the scene.

It's not the world tuning out the child, it's the child tuning out the world, she thought. To her, it's only as big as this train carriage, three and a half metres by thirty. Poorly oxygenated air.

Fenna smiled at the girl. She felt like a cigarette.

I I

Fenna pinched Rahel's cheek. Turning to her sister, Rahel saw for a moment the child she had once been – the chatterbox, as Verena had affectionately called her, as well as her little hussy.

There's another reason I'm here, Fenna whispered.

Let me sleep, said Rahel.

She closed her eyes again. A cloud passed across the sun, altering the light in the room.

Propping her head on her hand, Fenna looked at Leni. She stroked the girl's forehead, then Rahel's, and when Rahel at last opened her eyes, Fenna said, Mum has cancer.

No, said Rahel.

Breast cancer.

Rahel turned away. Suddenly she felt hot. Then she sat up, back to the wall.

She had an operation at the end of December, said Fenna. Three weeks later she started chemotherapy.

Rahel swallowed and shook her head. She looked down at Leni, still asleep, then back up at Fenna.

What's the prognosis?

Hard to say.

She didn't mention anything last time she was here.

She didn't want to heap more onto your plate. She got the diagnosis just before Leni was born.

Again, Rahel shook her head.

Her long hair, she said.

She wears a wig, said Fenna. And she's missed you, Rahel, all these years. Now more than ever.

Let's change the subject, said Rahel.

Do you have any idea how much she talked about you when I was living with her?

She didn't talk *to* me very much.

Give her a chance.

I'm suddenly supposed to go running back to her just because she's ill?

Doesn't have to be *back*. You can meet in the middle.

I'm not interested in hypocrisy, Rahel said.

Fenna settled her head on the pillow.

Wouldn't it be nice to put an end to this cold war once and for all? she asked.

Rahel ran her palms down her legs and clasped her ankles.

I just can't deal with her.

She's your mother, said Fenna.

Yeah, and what would you know about that?

Don't you think you're projecting a bit, that maybe you expected too much from her? I mean, said Fenna, she worked so hard for us.

Let it go, Rahel said firmly.

And yet you've stayed in touch, despite everything.

A few calls. Brief meet-ups. We've never had much common ground.

You're so harsh on yourself, so you're also harsh on Verena.

Rahel's gaze kept returning to Leni, who had put her thumb in her mouth and was sucking noisily.

How much do you know about her illness? she said.

Like I said, it's breast cancer. The operation went well, as far as these things can. The chemo ended a few days ago, but she may still need radiotherapy.

Is Inge looking after her? asked Rahel.

They see each other pretty much every day. Like always.

Taking Rahel's hand, Fenna went on: Maybe Mum would come down here for a couple of days.

You don't really believe that.

Would you be be up for it?

Rahel withdrew her hand.

If she really wants to come, she can.

I'll give her a call later, said Fenna.

Rahel reached for the duvet and pulled it up over Leni's small legs.

Did you get these from Mum? Fenna pointed at the bottom shelf of the bookcase next to the bed. On it was a stack of a dozen or so books.

She brought them for me a few weeks ago, Rahel said. The usual Verena stuff. Body, pregnancy, flowers, trees. One about the last ancient forests in Switzerland. It's really beautiful. In the beginning there was nothing but stone, ancient soil, chalky sediment.

Fenna put her arm around Rahel, drawing her closer.

Do you remember how Mum used to read to us? Night after night. The way she smelled the books as she opened them.

Slowly, Rahel shook her head.

Then she'd turn off the light, and I'd think: Don't go, Mum. I think I used to nod off after a couple of minutes anyway, especially if I asked her to make me another cup of tea. The sound of her busy in the kitchen, opening the cupboard, closing the cupboard, water splashing, the lid clinking against the pot.

How long do they think she's had cancer? asked Rahel.

It hasn't spread, as far as they can tell.

I don't remember the tea you're talking about either, said Rahel after a short silence. But I do remember something else. I remember a silly night when the three of you were merrily chatting away over the food. I remember the smell of fried eggs, of Inge's perfume – of Erik's clothes in the air. Disgusting.

She'd already taken them in and washed them by that point, said Fenna.

But she wore his clothes, said Rahel. Every day.

That's not the point. The problem is that you've forgotten all the little signs of affection she showed us – including you.

It definitely wasn't as romantic as you're describing, countered Rahel.

Those late-night visits from Verena's admirers were romantic, don't you remember? asked Fenna, laughing. She shagged her way through half the neighbouring villages like some horny teenager to prove she could have sex with men, not just with Inge. She even admitted it later.

You see, said Rahel, that's what I mean.

You've turned into a real prude, you know, said Fenna.

No. Just a mother.

You gave up at some point, didn't you? You're completely dependent on Boris. You go slinking off into your dream world, and then when you come to Zurich for literally the first time in three years you don't even let us know.

I had to see Maya, said Rahel.

Oh yeah? To see your little singing buddy? You haven't been in touch for ages. Not since you quit music and started denying that part of yourself.

Right, and you feel totally, completely independent of Luc, do you? That's why you're holed up here with me?

Fenna crouched down in front of Rahel. For a moment, Rahel thought she was about to lunge at her, but then Fenna tilted her pelvis back, slid both legs over the edge of the bed and stood up.

Is Boris cooking tonight? Or should I?

Rahel grabbed Fenna's shirt.

Shall I tell you something? she spat. You're just as dependent on Luc as Verena was on Erik. What are you going to do if he rejects you and the baby? You'll be working yourself to the bone like our mother did, and the kid will always come second.

Fenna turned, mingled amazement and disgust in her eyes.

I've got plenty of people in my life who think the same way I do, she said curtly.

Great, said Rahel. And yet you'll still be the one saddled with the responsibility. Or do you think your friends will spend all night pacing around the flat with a screaming baby, washing its shit out of your clothes and keeping everybody fed, purely out of the goodness of their hearts?

Like Boris did for you.

That's a completely different thing. We're married!

Your problem is that you can't think outside your rigid box, hissed Fenna.

Now Rahel stood up too. They faced each other.

Fine, then from now on you can talk to Verena about your kid.

She doesn't know I'm pregnant.

I bet in the end you'll wind up at hers, Rahel went on. As soon as she's better. Then the two of you will have it back, your household of women. Assuming the baby is a girl.

Suddenly Leni started to bawl, her eyes wide. Rahel picked her up, opened the door and called out for Rico. He appeared at the top of the attic stairs, holding a toy car. He waved to Rahel. Then he hopped down the steps, his hair flying with every jump.

Fenna put her hand on Rahel's back.

You've really got a problem, she said, more gently than Rahel would have liked.

I 2

Rahel lay down on the double bed and shut her eyes. Since Leni's birth nearly five months earlier, they had settled into a new nightly routine: in two or three hours Rico would slip into their bed, and Boris would move over to his. Later, after she had been breastfed, Leni would be taken out of her cot to curl up with Boris. Rahel switched off the bedside lamp and stretched out on the bed. Boris was still in his study.

After he came back from his trip, the five of them had spent the rest of the afternoon going for a walk in the forest. Fenna was unusually quiet, and Rahel didn't say much either. She remembered the day she'd moved in with Boris and he'd picked her up from the train station in his battered Toyota. He had been standing there with a bunch of orange and yellow tulips in his right hand and an unopened can of beer in the left, his shoulder-length hair wet with rain and clinging flat to the broad back of his head.

Come on, I'll drive us home, he'd called to her, gesturing broadly towards his car.

Three tulip petals had sailed to the ground and another three dropped as she greeted him with a hug; she was filled with heady joy. Boris smelled pleasantly of wood, mixed with the faint scent of alcohol. She only realised he'd had more than a sip when he started the car and the engine stalled twice.

Should I drive? asked Rahel, holding Boris's now open can of beer; she had put the flowers on the back seat.

Nah, it's fine, he replied, and burst into an abrupt guffaw.

He smacked the wheel with both fists and rocked his torso back and forth. Then he went quiet and looked Rahel straight in the eye.

I'm really sorry, he said. I was so nervous.

Rahel held out the can of beer.

I'll drive, she said, opening the passenger-side door.

Before she got out, Boris gave her hand a quick squeeze.

I've been really looking forward to seeing you, he said.

Rahel hadn't missed Maya, her friend from music school, for a single second, despite the fact that they'd lived together before she moved in with Boris and that Maya used to call her sis. As Rahel had become more and more visibly pregnant she'd used the word less and less, and her first comment when Rahel revealed she was moving in with Boris in the countryside, into a house surrounded by forest, had been: I guess you're serious, then, my erstwhile sister-in-song.

Rahel hugged the pillow; Boris's scent and hers had become one over the years, at least in this bed. The children were still sound asleep and Rahel tried to remember how she had pictured Boris's house before, but what popped into her head was the house from her dreams, the house with many rooms of her own design, which she reached down an unlit corridor. It was the house she had first dreamt of shortly after Erik left: vast, weighty, mutable. Night after night she opened every single one of the many doors, and behind one of them she had always found her father. The midge, as Verena had taken to calling him.

Ever since Erik slammed their front door behind him, Rahel had felt a piece of him on the inside, somehow. One of his legs had made her skin itch – her toes, the backs of her knees, her scalp – and she'd often had the same feeling in her belly, to the left of her stomach. It was an itch that sometimes came over her unexpectedly in the middle of class, but also when she was alone and couldn't sleep at night. She sang 'A Little Man Stands in the Forest', 'Frère Jacques' and 'Green, Green, Green' to reassure herself, and after a while she saw it as a kind of training, to not give in to the itch and never to scratch. The day after Erik left, Rahel had started looking for flying insects, keeping them trapped in a jam jar in her room until they died. Then she plucked off all but one of their legs and buried every single one around the house where she lived with Verena and Fenna.

Years later, shortly after arriving at college, Rahel heard the song for the first time. She and her then boyfriend Chris, a fellow music student, had eaten dinner after a long rehearsal before dozing off on the threadbare sofa in his shared flat, her head resting in his lap. Suddenly she became aware of a melody, a song moving deep within, and she woke languidly, as though in a dream, to music that was calm yet urgent, sung by a clear female voice. By the time it was over, Rahel was wide awake and saying: Play that one more time. The song began with the English words 'Daddy Longleg', but apart from that she paid no attention to the lyrics. It peeled open a feeling inside her that she hadn't known before; it wasn't about Chris, who was still lying on – he seemed oddly far away, with his serious face – and yet her feelings for him, for the man, intensified in that moment. She lay there motionless, feeling his warm legs under her head, the scent of laundry detergent, jeans and sex in her nostrils, and was happy and sad at the same time.

It wasn't until weeks later, after she'd played the song a few times without prompting the same emotion as on her first listening, that she googled the lyrics. The words were abstract, unmoored. She didn't know what Daddy Longleg meant, but the search engine translated it for her: *winged insect*, it spat out. *See crane fly, mosquito, midge*.

Rahel remembered that as a child she had mainly pictured a wild, overgrown beard after her father left, because in the two photos she had of him, it was almost impossible to make out anything except his tangled whiskers. She had to stare at the photographs for ages until she could see Erik clearly again, so she was amazed how vividly he appeared before her as she listened to 'Daddy Longleg' over and over again, sometimes for hours on repeat. Eventually the words 'where he's sheltered from growing old' got stuck in her brain, and in a heartbeat it grew clear to her that the time had finally come to bid her dad goodbye.

At the end of her first year she started writing her own lyrics. Day and night she paced the unlit corridor of her inner house, searching for the room where her father sat. In the meantime she painted his beard in a panoply of colours – red, violet, green – and atmospheric, practically wordless pieces emerged. Eventually, Rahel was ready to add more lyrics, redrawing her father anew: as a carpenter travelling across the world, dressed in flares and a broad-brimmed hat; as a guru at the head of his own sect, with long black locks; as a rat; as a pimp in Cuba with a walrus moustache.

Rahel sang. She performed with her band in bars and small clubs, or at student parties. She raised her voice in front of her audience, unstoppably in motion: songs collected inside her, pouring out onto paper. Songs in her voice.

When she was nine years old, she wrote to him. In the space of a year, she gave Verena three letters, asking her to send them to Erik. She was always afraid of her mother's eyes, which began to flash darkly whenever Rahel said the words father or Erik; and she was afraid of her sentences, which could be like the points of knives. Rahel knew that her father had come to Switzerland from northern Germany to work on the railway. He had been a tall man, a gentle person at first, according to Verena. She spoke calmly and in detail about Erik only once, on the day Rahel got her first period. After Fenna had gone to sleep, Verena pulled a tiny bottle of advocaat out of her handbag and filled two small glasses. Clinking hers against Rahel's, she whispered:

You're a woman now.

Rahel had smiled. She'd have preferred to be in bed, reading.

You know, your father and I were night and day, Verena had abruptly started to explain. Neither of us was able to hug the other anymore. We were husband and wife, back to back. It's hard to believe that between us we made you and Fenna. It's good. But he wouldn't have known what to do with two daughters. All he could do was walk out.

Rahel had nodded, sipping at her glass. Verena poured herself another and kept talking, telling her that Erik had eventually emigrated from northern Germany to Asia, or to South America, she wasn't exactly sure.

From then on, for Rahel, Erik was trapped in the letter P, in its small arc, standing on one leg in Pyongyang or Palembang, in Porto Alegre. As a student, whenever she was onstage singing her songs about a father, she bid him, bid his image, goodbye.

Then, end of her second year, his letter had arrived. Two pages, Erik sent her, one dense with type and the other only a quarter full. The three-quarter emptiness of the second page had mirrored her own, which she could feel even as she read the words: Hello Rahel. The letter seemed to consist of nothing but bald type. Her heart thudded wildly as she tried to pick up Erik's scent, reading the lines in which he told her he'd got her album through a friend but had found the music boring. Structureless, he called it. The sax was fine but the lyrics were terrible, perverse. All that stuff about a 'father' she had pictured as a guru, a pimp, a penguin was, he assumed, her way of trying to get her own back. He was appalled by Rahel's career path, he said, by the fact that she seemed to have the same nasty personality as her mother, who would no doubt have told her quite bizarre things about him. He wished her a pleasant life. Goodbye.

Rahel had run her fingers over the German stamps on the envelope, and as she imagined going to meet this unknown father, wherever he lived, looking into his face and lashing out at it, the next moment she thought of her mother, sitting on the floor on silly nights, her fingers in a pot full of soft-boiled eggs. In her mind Rahel was above Verena, casting a shadow over her mother; Verena laughed brightly, looking Rahel full in the face.

She sat up with a jolt. Her lips were painful. She opened her mouth as wide as she could three times then glanced at Leni, asleep in her cot with her little arms outstretched. Her nostrils quivered with each breath. Rahel plumped up the pillow, settled back down, shut her eyes and let herself drift on, remembering how she'd put the letter on her desk and tried to get hold of Chris. When he didn't pick up, she texted. For a while she had padded uneasily through her studio apartment, holding the two pages of the letter, placing them on the bookshelf, under the candlestick, next to the bedside table, on the stack of newspapers. Whenever she picked them up it made her shudder, so she decided to destroy them and tell nobody but Chris.

She walked down to the River Aare by herself, that same chilly November afternoon. I've got to plant positive thoughts in my mind, she was thinking, and she kept laughing softly – at herself, at the fact that she'd brought nothing with her but this ridiculous letter, a small bottle of hard liquor and a lighter. When she reached the Aare, she opened the bottle, shook the alcohol over the paper and set it alight. The fire went out as quickly as it kindled. Instead of the paper, Rahel burned the fingers of her right hand. Bending down, she dipped them in the Aare. The water was ice cold. Still, she held them in the languid current and imagined pulling out a different hand, a royal blue hand much bigger than before, one with a new lifeline drawn. Then she crumpled up the letter with numb fingers and threw it into the river. Slowly she trudged back up to the city centre. She bought some hot tea and a sandwich at a cafeteria, sat down at a table in the glaring light and ate. Her phone pinged. A message from Chris.

You're a magnificent artist, he wrote. Powerful. I'm proud of you.

Rahel sat there for a few more minutes, gazing at the phone as a prickling sensation spread throughout her chest. By the time she left the restaurant, the prickling had reached her hand as well; it felt large and heavy now, a paw, and she would never forget that image of a hand, she thought. She would buy a glove for her right hand two sizes too big, brandish her right fist if anyone ever threatened her. She would tend the positive thoughts in her mind with that hand. Water them, pluck off their dry leaves.

Long before she met Boris, Erik had shrunk from his motley roles back down into an insect. She had performed a few of the songs about him for several more years, until she left college. After that, the daddy longlegs had lingered only as a faint memory, almost sweet. There were plenty of them at Boris's house. Rahel caught each one in an empty jam jar and put them behind the well outside.

She turned from left to right, from right to left; the duvet cover rustled. Heaving herself to her feet, she fumbled through the unlit room, went down the dark hall and into the bathroom. It was only in such moments late at night that she felt almost as though she was in the house she had once wanted. Bunching up her nightgown, she sat down on the toilet.

At first, in Gesswil, she'd still listened to 'Daddy Longleg' occasionally. The song had reminded her not just of her father but of Chris, of his smell, of fleeting moments of happiness. They were moments of not-yet and no-more, Rico's birth being one of them. At the delivery, Rahel had found herself in a dark corridor of gleaming black walls, an opening that was deep within her yet somehow external. She had felt something similar back when she used to write songs, when the melodies were already in her head but not yet on paper, as she shaped the notes in her mouth, just before they escaped. She had become Eve, pale and vulnerable like Dürer's, but with a strong will and the urge to create. To fashion something new.

Rahel flushed the toilet. Again she was groping down the corridor, pausing outside a glistening purple door. She opened it. For a split second, Maya's face appeared right in front of her. It was contorted into a grimace. She heard a loud noise like a balloon popping, then everything went black. She strained to see something, anything, in the room, twisting her head from side to side, pushing further and further until she could swivel it 360 degrees; her vision swirled and suddenly she noticed that a corner of the room was illuminated. There lay Eve, under a garish neon light. Rahel went over and looked into her face, which was her own, with its lips sewn shut. Her mouth twitched, the thread pulled taut, her lips stretched, thin threads of vomit ran down her chin and cheeks; Rahel started awake.

She was cowering in the corner of her study, a stack of paper in front of her. First, she ran her hand gingerly over her undamaged lips, then over the pile: German weeklies and free regional newspapers, flyers and fashion catalogues, two dog-eared, empty notebooks. After a few minutes she stood up and crept into the kitchen for a sip or two of water, straight from the tap. Briefly she stopped outside Fenna's bedroom door and listened. Silence. Finally she got back into her bed, which had gone cold.

13

Some weeks before Fenna arrived, Rahel had dreamt of a large, high stage. She was standing in front of it. Black floor, black curtains, black ceiling, and a sharp wind that whistled unpleasantly in her ears. In the middle of the stage, at head height, was Leni, flat on her back and screaming with all her might. Rahel opened her mouth and sang, but her own voice seemed to come from another room, muffled and far too quiet; she grabbed her throat and when she opened her eyes, she recognised the low wooden ceiling above her. She looked at the alarm clock: 6.52 a.m. Her throat prickled.

Softly, so as not to wake anyone else, she got up and pulled on her thick cotton trousers and woollen jumper. In the kitchen she poured ground coffee into the funnel of the espresso maker, tamped it down and set it on the stove. She poured the coffee into a thermos and stuffed it into her rucksack along with two slices of bread. Only when she stepped out through the front door did she notice the dense mist. Turning back, she went to fetch her raincoat from the peg. She'd had it fifteen years, and these days when she wore it in the rain she was soaked to the skin within minutes. But it was good enough for mist.

Rahel tried to remember the last time she'd been outside alone. Rico sometimes led her purposefully towards the new housing estate so he could play at the playground there, or to the Niedermanns', the family on the farm next door. That was where his best friend lived. Lukas. Often, too, he led her into the forest to look for bird's nests or to climb up into the raised hide. It was roughly one metre by one and a half, with grass-green hatches that opened on three sides. The bench along the wall overlooked a clearing; the forest trail passed behind the hide, but when you were sitting on the bench you felt utterly secluded.

Rahel set off across the muddy field towards the hide. A fifteen-minute walk, if you were brisk. Birds sang loudly. She shivered. Her nipples hurt – they'd been sore again for days from the extra breastfeeding.

Pausing in the middle of the field, she dug two tissues out of her rucksack, laid them for a moment in the damp grass then tucked them into her bra. They cooled her breasts. Rahel glanced around. She could see barely three metres, white on white, only the greenish-brown earth standing firm against the vanishing landscape. Just vanish, vanish, she thought. She bent down again and dug her index finger into the soil. Cool, wet, placid. Leni would soon be wanting her morning feed.

Rahel got up, examined her brown finger then looked again at the white curtain of mist. The way to the heart is through the stomach, she thought, and pictured again what her body was producing: the watery fluid they called mother's milk. The lactation specialist at the hospital had assured her there was love in it, that it was the best thing for the baby, but Rahel was convinced her milk wasn't doing Leni good. Lovely white milk – but not hers, not Rahel's, and breastfeeding her baby wasn't an act of love: it hurt enough to make her scream.

That she loved him had been her first clear thought when she met Boris. He had driven her to euphoria with that caring look in his eyes. Rahel had sensed early on that he was someone to be relied on. But that reliability had crumbled in recent months. Twice Boris had stayed out all night, five times the whole day. He'd tell her where he was going beforehand, looking at her as though waiting for her to ask more questions. Something in Rahel's throat had tightened at those moments. She had nodded and tried to smile. A few hours away, she thought, that's fine. That's got to be fine.

One night when Boris was out, Rahel had taken her phone and looked up one of the little clips she'd once called porn. She had watched one for the first time in her life when she was seven months pregnant with Rico. Waking up alone in Maya's Zurich flat with a tickle low in her abdomen, she had switched on her phone but found nothing but over-aestheticised fucking. In every clip, the woman was grabbed and taken by the man, presented to the camera, moaning and play-acting lust. The couple didn't look at one another, a strange mixture of presence and indifference between the two of them, and between the couple and the camera. Her urge satisfied, Rahel's desire abruptly drained away. She lay on her side, the child in her belly quite still. As she fast-forwarded through the rest of the recording, she kept wondering why this cheap porn always ended with the man kneeling over the woman and one of them rubbing his penis until it squirted semen.

Towards the end of her pregnancy, when Rahel had already met Boris, she stopped watching the films. But that night, with the children in bed and Boris somewhere else, she gazed soberly at the doctor's-office whiteness of the porn. She was missing something, she realised with painful awareness. But what? At some point Boris would leave, she thought. It would be easy for him, without the burden of motherhood.

As Rahel walked through the early-morning April mist, she realised all at once what Boris saw in spending time away from home. Just setting out. Being free. She inhaled deeply, her lungs becoming damp and heavy. She had hardly reached the forest before she was surrounded by tall spruces, motionless in the haze, heedless in their rich green. She went up to the hide and climbed the ladder. At the top she coughed, spitting phlegm onto the grass below. The trees on the other side of the clearing were visible only in outline. Rahel took out her thermos and poured herself a coffee. She blew gently on the steaming drink. It had been so long since she had really sung, she thought; her singing voice was as distant as in the dreams she had night after night. Ever since she'd stopped, when Rico was barely a year old, she had done nothing more than occasionally, while cleaning, leaf through the scores she kept in the desk drawer in her study, and she always swiftly put them back.

Rahel took a sip of coffee. It was too bitter. Her throat felt scratchy. She cleared it and spat again. She wanted to sing again at long last, but not a single piece of music came to mind, no jazz standards, none of her own compositions, no nursery rhymes. She sang a loud, high note. It sounded unusually bright and lovely, her voice.

Rahel took a notebook out of her rucksack. There was nothing written in it, only the picture of Eve that Chris had sent her, which she had tucked between the pages a little while back. Rahel had stumbled across it in the cardboard box of Fenna's letters, and looked up *Eve* and *Dürer* on the web. That was when she'd discovered there were actually two parts to the painting. Dürer had also painted an Adam. He was touching a branch with his index and middle fingers, and on the branch grew an apple, an orange-red fruit. Leaves covered his genitals. His mouth was slightly parted, his cheeks soft. He looked like he was about to apologise for something he was now ashamed of; his fine curls seemed lifted by the wind. If his build and especially his chest hadn't been so distinctly masculine, Rahel would have thought she was looking into the face of a woman. She had printed out the picture in colour and cut out Adam's head, pasting it next to Eve. 'Eve and A.' was the name of her new creation.

Rahel sang another note, deeper this time. Finally she broke off.

She screwed the top on the thermos and put it back in her rucksack with the empty notebook. Then she left the forest in the opposite direction. From a distance she could already see the new housing estate, where she would catch the bus to Gesswil and from there the train. She wanted to be elsewhere. She wanted to be far away.

14

The train to Germany, a boat into the distance. That was the route her father had travelled, at least according to Verena, and the train rolled on; Rahel's eyes stayed closed at first, particles of light dancing on her lids, like little dotted words that swelled into Verena's question, the question she had asked in every one of her rare phone calls after Rico's birth, putting her emphasis on the word in the middle: Does your son make you happy?

Rahel had always had the same answer: That child is my greatest joy.

She opened her eyes. The landscape was passing by outside. Slipping off her shoes, she placed her feet on the upholstery in front of her, set her backpack on one free seat and her rain jacket on the other. Maya, she thought, I'm coming back now. She would immerse herself in the past like a warm, bubbling bath, Rahel was sure of it. Sing again. Write again.

PART TWO

To print the cursed kiss upon you, catch you with my mouth, my tongue.
Daughter, tone, daughter, tone; I'm falling,

the body halved before me, each half trapping notes that do not sound.

There I lie, scattered among my children.

I

Inge parked the car outside Boris and Rahel's house. The rounded top of the conker tree was nebulous in the twilight, blurring slowly into the darkening sky. She took one large and one small bag out of the boot, set them down beside the car and swung her black braid onto her back. Rahel stepped outside, her cardigan wrapped tightly around her body. She took small steps towards the car. Inge waved, her whole frame seemingly in motion. Rahel lifted her arm and waved back. The passenger door opened. Slowly, Verena placed her feet on the ground, straightened her trunk, raised her backside off the seat and stood to face Rahel: tired, dull eyes in a face that seemed very small, red hair flopping haphazardly on her head. Rahel took her hand; bony and cold. For a brief moment she felt like shoving her stooped mother back into the dark interior of the car. She would have closed the door, spun on her heel and walked back into the house alone, into her home. Rahel stood motionless. She let go of her mother's hand, then gave her a cursory hug.

Mum! shouted Fenna, who had also come outside. She paused in front of Verena as though to briefly gather herself, then pulled her cautiously close. She greeted Inge in the same way.

Good journey? asked Rahel.

Inge nodded. Not much traffic, a magnificent sunset.

The four of them fell silent for a minute. A watchful

speechlessness swung back and forth between them, glances, Fenna's smile. Inge's breathing was very audible.

Would you like to come in too? asked Rahel.

Inge said she'd love to, but the return journey would take at least an hour and a half, and she was already pretty tired.

Rahel was about to say something when Boris appeared behind her and said hello to the two women – much too loudly, Rahel thought. She turned slightly away from him and looked at Fenna, who now stood next to Verena, arm in arm, a familiar sight. It had changed slowly but clearly over the years: Fenna towered over her mother by a good twenty centimetres now, plump cheeks threaded with fine red veins that Rahel could only imagine in the half-gloom. Verena wore a thin hip-length coat. Her eyes focused on her surroundings: the gravel, the field, the treetops, the house and finally Rahel; their eyes met, and something that made Rahel shudder flashed across Verena's face. For a fraction of a second she saw herself in it; she was this person, this gaunt figure, her mother's guarded affection. Rahel scraped her foot across the ground.

Inge soon said her goodbyes. She gave Verena a long hug, while Boris carried the bags into the house and Fenna and Rahel stood a little to one side. By now it was quite dark; bats flitted through the air. Then Fenna and Verena set off towards the house. Inge lingered with Rahel and said that Verena was glad to be alone with them. She told Rahel she'd visit her some other time – it had been too long, and she'd love to finally meet the children.

She hugged Rahel the way she'd hugged Verena earlier, only not as long, and silently this time. She'd said something quietly to Verena, with emphasis; Rahel could tell even though she didn't catch the words. The whisper had startled the falling night and her own unease. It had mingled with the sounds of spring, with the wind, which had picked up, and with the song of a few solitary blackbirds and robins.

Inge got into the car and started the engine, the gravel crunching under her tyres as she drove away. Fenna, standing in the doorway, gave Rahel a wave.

I'm so pleased she's here.

Fenna ran her hand through her hair. She smelled to Rahel of sweet shampoo.

Rahel opened every window, starting on the ground floor and working her way up. Verena would have the guest room where Fenna had spent two nights, and Fenna had already moved into the smallest room in the house, which had previously been used as a box room and which they had cleaned out together that afternoon. They carried all sorts of things that hadn't been used for years over to the barn: decorative knick-knacks, worn-out shoes, unused furniture. Fenna's room was left with the bare essentials: a mattress with fresh sheets, a bedside table and a shelf. That would do her just fine, Fenna had said, it was only for sleeping anyway. Rico, his mouth full of rice, had announced at dinner that he was moving too, into his playroom in the attic. Rahel thought she caught a brief glimpse of triumph on Boris's face. After brushing his teeth, Rico took his blanket out of the family bedroom and gazed at Rahel expectantly as he waited on the landing. With Boris's help she had moved his bed upstairs, lingering in his playroom for a while as he allocated his stuffed mouse, bear and sheep new spots on the bed, explaining to them that they had their own domain now. As always, Rahel read him a picture book, pressed a kiss onto his forehead and wished him goodnight. When she had left the room, she swallowed hard; he had moved out. From now on, her boy would sleep in the room above hers.

When the window was open in Boris's study, too, Rahel went back downstairs and closed window after window. Spring is in the house now, she thought, its scent has settled on the bedclothes, on the bookshelves, the carpets, pictures, tables, on Rico's toys and in her clothes, and she hoped it had also gathered in the cracks in the wood and sealed them, so that the rooms would be less porous.

Verena, Fenna and Boris were in the living room with Leni, who was now wide awake. Rahel held her to her breast. She took her evening feed, drinking greedily at first, then more and more slowly until her soft snores drifted through the room. Verena, Boris and Fenna chatted in a whisper about the trip to Gesswil, the spruce forests around the house, breakfast plans for the next day.

I'll put Leni to bed, Rahel said, getting up.

I'm tired too, said Verena.

Would you like another glass of water? A bite to eat? asked Boris, pushing his empty can of beer aside.

Something to fill my hot-water bottle would be nice, Verena said, but otherwise sleep is all I need.

As Rahel was changing Leni in her bedroom one more time, she heard Verena and Fenna in the bathroom, a soft murmuring, the scrape of teeth being brushed, gurgling, the tap. Coming out of the bedroom, she found Verena in the dark corridor. Her face still seemed small, but it had regained a certain fullness.

Rahel?

Yes?

Thank you for letting me stay.

Rahel took a slight step backwards.

Of course, she replied dully.

Verena touched her shoulder with the pads of her fingers as Boris came trudging heavily up the stairs and handed Verena the bright red hot-water bottle.

Good night, she said.

Good night, answered Rahel and Boris in unison.

Boris, Fenna and Rahel sat back down at the table in the living room.

I've been thinking about going on a trip, said Boris. With the kids. For two days.

Rahel fixed her eyes on him, the hollows underneath strikingly dark.

Why? she asked.

There's not much room here for four adults and two kids, said Fenna, jumping in.

Rahel leant back in the armchair. The padding grew softer and softer until she thought she might be swallowed up. She clutched tightly at the armrests, and suddenly Boris was arrayed in manifold form before her eyes, kaleidoscopic images, but not colourful; they were drab and blurred.

Could do, she said hastily.

She avoided Boris's gaze and stretched out her arm instead, wanting to touch him, his warm flesh, the moles and fine hairs on his forearm. To keep him with her. But at the last moment she reached purposefully for his can of beer, which was still on the table, and flattened it with both hands.

Alright, she said. Off to bed.

Before she went to sleep, Rahel went down into the cellar and examined the jars. Damson plums, all pale-red flesh and near-black skins, submarines in red wine; next, the jars of bright pears, glowing in their cinnamon-and-sugar water; and then the mixed vegetables, yellow, white, green splashes of colour. Beside the pickles and preserves she had made were jars of pesto and boxes of pasta, one shelf of wine, one of beer, and two boxes at the bottom that contained potatoes and carrots. Rahel tucked under her arm a jar of gooseberry jam, which Boris loved, and two jars of apple sauce. All at once she felt like talking. She went upstairs, deposited the jars in the kitchen, went into the bathroom, brushed her teeth, padded quietly into the bedroom, pulled on her nightdress and got into bed next to Boris. Words floated through her head, but she was too tired to catch hold of them. Resting her chest hesitantly against Boris, hands and arms by her sides, like his, she slept soundly for the first three hours of the night.

2

She looked up. The tall building with the familiar *hotel banana city* sign passed by outside, her train pulled in at Winterthur moments later, and Rahel could have got off at the station, walked through town and found a café somewhere. She stayed seated, upright. She'd been pumped full of adrenaline ever since leaving the hide and catching the bus in Gesswil, like a child taking the train alone for the first time. She was travelling by herself, which she hadn't done in more than three years. The train set off again with a judder. Her stomach contracted and released with a prickle. A runaway. A truant. Boris had no idea where she was. All she knew was that she was going to Zurich, to the urban world she had left behind just over three years ago, after living there for a few months, when she had roamed block after block with Maya, searching everywhere for a non-alcoholic drink while Maya knocked back vodka and coke and Campari and orange and Rahel's rounded belly was given the occasional narrow-eyed stare.

Maya, the pretty one, with collarbones like bass clefs turned aslant. She had finished her studies at the same time as Rahel, and had barely left college before she was singing at all the hottest clubs in Switzerland, as well as at KKL and Moods, the major festivals and on the hippest stages in Berlin. Unlike Rahel, Maya had moved away from classical jazz while they were still in training, drifting in the direction of pop, which audiences liked: wherever she sang, she drew a crowd. Research trips, Maya called her excursions with Rahel; she wrote songs about Zurich's front gardens, its suburbs, the areas around train stations.

A jolt of pain ran through Rahel. Her breasts were clamouring for relief. At Zurich Airport a man in a suit hauled his shiny silver suitcase off the luggage rack and left the train. Other passengers got onto the escalator and glided upwards into the departures terminal.

A young man sat down opposite Rahel. He wore a black beanie that didn't cover his ears and a moustache. His cheeks and chin shone as though no hair had ever sprouted there, lending a touch of irony to the moustache.

Where do people hang out in Zurich these days? asked Rahel.

The young man gave her a quizzical look, pulling the earbuds out of his ears.

What?

Where do people go in Zurich these days?

No idea. Café Lang for coffee. Or Zum Guten Glück.

Brushing his index finger over his moustache, he prepared to devote himself once more to his music.

And where else? asked Rahel quickly.

He paused, one earbud clamped between his index and middle fingers.

You've not really got out much in a while, huh?

Exactly. I'm Rahel. Can you take me somewhere?

He glanced briefly out of the window, then back at her. Then he shook his head.

No time, sorry.

I'll give you the time.

He shook his head again and stuffed the earbuds into his ears. Rahel laughed out loud and turned to look outside.

Minutes later, the train arrived at Zurich's main station. Rahel smiled at the young man before she left the carriage. She'd get a studio, she thought, as she stepped out onto the platform. Partner up with Maya again. Hang out in cafés. She got purposefully onto the tram and rode it to Schörlistraße. There she got out, the motorway roaring at her back, and the grey sky stretched above her as the clouds parted here and there. It was all still there: the bold FCZ graffiti, the grey, pink and beige apartment blocks, the rows of garages. Walking past Loosli, the car repair place, Rahel caught sight of her silhouette in the workshop's tall windows. She stopped abruptly and turned ninety degrees. She was wearing her frowsy tracksuit bottoms and old woollen jumper, which oozed out from underneath the too-short sleeves of her rain jacket. The pale blue of the jacket was impossible to make out in the glass – only the reflective strips which caught the light. As she eyed her gaunt figure, Rahel remembered what Maya had said to her at the main station in Bern, when she had been nine weeks pregnant, swaying with nausea and even scrawnier than usual because she threw up every meal:

Rahel, you look a fraction of yourself.

Well, now she'd come to get the rest of herself back. She grinned at her reflection. Then she turned away and ducked down Tulpenweg. The main door at number twelve was unlocked. Rahel went up to the second floor and rang the bell.

Silence. From a floor further up came the heavy buzz of a drill, which soon broke off once more. She tried again, then again, Morse code with no one to receive it. All at once she was exhausted. She let herself slide down the door onto the ground and wrapped her arms around her knees.

3

Mother in my house, before — behind — beside; I lie cramped, child's head on my breast, pursed lips. At night you seek the milk with your hands.

4

Leni woke her with a cry of protest. Rahel jumped; she'd had no idea how late it was. She had woken up in the night, lips throbbing, and groped her way down the hall into the bathroom, examined her face for a few minutes in the mirror, then come back and gone straight to sleep. At some point she'd woken up again with dream-like images of a narrow balcony overgrown with moss in her mind's eye; Verena was there too, shadowy, waving at her in slow motion. She had breastfed Leni, lying down with her notebook open and scrawling a few words. At first the sharp tug at her breast had hurt. The girl was too big, clinging to her like glue, but the more letters she wrote the softer the pencil on the paper, and the more she softened herself. Now it was already light in the room, and Boris's side of the bed was empty. On the table was the book about the last ancient Swiss forest, which she had put there the day before.

Rock mass, *karstification*, *hydrology*; she muttered the words to herself as she fed the girl. Then she put on some clothes. From downstairs she heard footsteps and voices. The others must already be awake.

She bumped into her sister on the stairs.

Good morning, sleepyhead, said Fenna. We've already had breakfast and we're meeting in Verena's room in twenty minutes. You coming?

Rahel nodded. Leni was heavy in her arms; downstairs, Verena was carrying crumb-strewn plates into the kitchen from the living room, Boris following. Rico came upstairs and cuddled up against her legs.

Hello Mummy.

In the kitchen, Rahel put Leni in the baby swing, opened a jar of apple sauce, poured some into a small bowl and spooned in some yoghurt. Boris sat opposite. Rico was babbling to himself on the floor, scooping the air with a toy digger. Upstairs, they heard the patter of the shower.

We didn't want to wake you, said Boris.

Rahel finished her bowl, grabbed a slice of bread and spread it with butter and honey. She was hungrier than she'd been in ages.

That's fine, she murmured.

For the second time she poured herself a coffee, added plenty of milk and emptied the cup in one gulp.

Everything alright? asked Boris.

If I were you, I'd probably need a beer, Rahel said.

Got it, said Boris, making a serious face.

Rahel stared into the cup. A greyish-white drop of milky coffee had collected at the bottom.

You're stressed about me going away with the kids, Boris said.

I miss you already, she answered promptly.

Who, Rico?

All three of you.

You were the one who wanted some distance, you know.

Was I?

You walked out! Without so much as a word.

I've explained that.

A test. You wanted to test something. But what? When are you finally going to tell me the whole truth?

You're leaving too.

Yeah, for two days. To see my parents, while you stay here and have fun with your guests.

After that you're leaving altogether, aren't you? After that you're getting the hell out of here.

Boris shook his head jerkily.

Give that stuff a fucking rest, he said.

Rahel wiped her palm across the table, sending breadcrumbs to the floor. She got up and reached for the hoover behind the door, then changed her mind, letting it go and coming to stand behind Boris's chair. She leant over him. For a moment, her hair grazed his forehead. He tried to clasp her wrist, but she was already straightening up.

Boris remained seated, his head propped in his hands, as Rahel brewed herbal tea, set a pot and three cups on a small tray and left the kitchen without another word.

Verena and Fenna were sitting on the floor in Verena's room. Rahel passed each of them a handle-less mug. After a brief hesitation, she sat down too and poured the tea. Sunlight slanted into the room, making Verena's red hair gleam. She seemed more awake than the night before. Her bags were at the foot of the bed; the smaller bag was unopened, but on the larger one were two folded jumpers and a toiletry bag. Rahel felt sick.

Did you sleep well? asked Verena.

Not bad. You guys?

Fine, answered Fenna.

Verena adjusted the woollen blanket draped over her knees and said: This is what I've always wanted. A couple of days together. Timeless. And well rested.

We did use to sit like this, said Fenna.

That was a long time ago, replied Verena. And in those days I was never well rested.

But it was so cosy, said Fenna. Scrambled eggs, a bit of bread, music, sitting on the soft carpet. That was all it took.

Rahel propped herself up on the floor.

Silly nights, she said dully. What a name.

Verena took a sip of tea and coughed as she put the mug back on the tray. A mint leaf floated to the surface of Rahel's mug. She followed it with her eyes as she asked: How are you really doing, Verena?

She looked at her mother, who shook her head and touched her left hand to her chest as though to forestall further questions.

And Inge?

She's keeping busy in the garden and with the hens, answered Verena. Last year the harvest was phenomenal – we're still eating the autumn crop of apples. She only works two days a week at the florist now. We'll often take a walk into the village, or I'll watch her turn over the soil, pull up the weeds, plant shrubs.

So you go outside? asked Rahel.

Of course. But a lot of the time I'm too tired. Fenna must have told you I'm on sick leave from work. They were very accommodating. Well, I mean, I've been working there for more than twenty-five years. Crazy.

We'll look after you now, said Fenna. You just rest.

You don't need to worry about me. I got through chemo – now it's just rads.

So you've got the worst behind you? asked Rahel.

Verena nodded.

So they tell me, anyway. They were able to remove the tumour without damaging the breast. They haven't found any metastases yet.

Must have been a difficult time for you. For both of you.

I don't know what I would have done without Inge, Verena said almost tonelessly.

She sat up, her shoulders faintly hunched. Rahel scrutinised her mother. She was noticeably older, more slender in stature, the deep lines carved anew, more angularly, and yet at the same time there was a lightness about her. Something she had always sought before was now apparent on her face, like a fine layer of powder: impartiality.

Rahel shuffled towards Verena and put her arm hesitantly around her shoulders; Verena's body felt hard. Suddenly there was an almost imperceptible trembling. Verena bent her head towards Rahel and laid her head against her – like the child, thought Rahel, that she must have been before she met Erik, before her belly rounded for the first time.

Verena said: I'm glad we're together. It's been a long time since we talked.

Yes, we should have a proper chat in the next few days, said Fenna. We should really let ourselves vent, because I need to hear from you guys. Rahel, you especially.

Rahel let Verena go.

But this isn't about me right now.

Yes it is, Fenna said. It's about you too.

I really need a drink, Rahel said. Not this herbal stuff, some decent schnapps, liqueur, rosé. Red wine in the evenings. First being pregnant, then breastfeeding. It's been way too long.

Go on, have a glass, said Verena, who had straightened up again. No one's going to be scandalised.

Rahel laughed scornfully.

Why am I not surprised? she said.

Will you tell me about Leni's birth? asked Verena.

There was a knock at the door. When it opened, Boris was standing in the doorframe. He wore a sleeveless shirt, his gut bulged over his jeans, and he was holding Leni to his chest with his left arm. Rico appeared behind him.

Alright, we're off, said Boris. We'll be back tomorrow night.

Rahel got up, kissed Rico and Leni on the forehead and wrapped her arms around Boris's neck. She hugged him, feeling choked. She pulled away, ashamed of her damp eyes, of being unable to swallow.

All packed? she asked in a shaking voice. Leni's powdered milk and the mash?

We'll be fine, said Boris.

OK, have fun then, whispered Rahel, tousling Rico's hair.

Aren't you coming? asked Rico, holding out his arms to her. She picked him up and put her cheek to his.

It's only for one night, said Rahel. You can sleep with Oma. I'll be thinking of you, I'll come and visit you in your dreams. And I bet you'll have that yummy strawberry yoghurt again for breakfast.

Rico nodded earnestly. Rahel put him down, both feet on the ground. Boris took his hand, said goodbye to Verena and Fenna, and left the room. Rahel shut the door behind them, catching a brief howl from Rico. She sat back down with legs of rubber, her throat still constricted, and the stinging spreading even further through her chest and around her mouth.

Your first night without Leni? asked Fenna.

Rahel nodded, quickly pressing her lips tight.

And the second without Rico.

You're a pretty hardcore mum.

Silence filled the room. Then Fenna gave a short, dazzling laugh.

And Rahel asked: What was it really like for you, when Erik left, I mean?

Outside they heard car doors slamming, then the engine starting.

It's been so long, Verena said. I think I was glad and bitter at the same time. It set me free, that's for sure. But it still hurt, and not just because he'd been such a support for me.

Financially? asked Rahel.

That too.

Is that why you're with Boris? asked Fenna, turning to Rahel.

For financial reasons? Rahel looked at her.

Because he's got your back, he supports you.

What kind of a question is that?

You've been happier, said Fenna.

Haven't we all?

What's wrong with you? asked Fenna. Why do you get so worked up?

Rahel picked at the nailbed on her right middle finger, then got to her feet and headed for the bedroom door before she stopped short.

5

Tired, with the little one on top of me, balled fists, warm tummy rising and falling, soft breaths, she turns her head. Leni. So peaceful. And I bear the inflammation in my breasts, in my throat, in my ears, inside my very head, where thoughts circle like feral dogs. Tired, but my legs carry me without effort, from my hip bones to my heels: unscathed. I splay my toes and touch them to the inside of my shoes. What wouldn't I give to lie for days, no child, no belly, no head? Asleep.

I let the hot water run over me, flushed skin. The door opens, I feel caught. It's Boris, mouth open, words slipping out inside speech bubbles. I read: You didn't cook, didn't clean, didn't change the baby, didn't iron, didn't do your make-up, didn't fuck. Nothing from you, nothing with you, wife, today!

I turn back and forth in the tub. The water is silvery and so hot it feels cold again, it's liquid aluminium, and a fine layer coats me like a second lustrous skin. Boris holds my head, bends over me, kisses my forehead, says: Your hair is ridiculous. I wake up. Lying in the dark. I don't move, I hear the children breathing, Bori's breathing, and in the end my breathing too. Astonishingly calm. I know I have milk inside me still, it must come out, out, it all must come out.

6

She stood a while in front of the closed bedroom door. The patterns in the wood were like drawings – dark eyes, hooked noses, strange ciphers. For a moment it felt to Rahel as though the floor were slipping away. She composed herself, but when she began to speak she seemed somehow in a trance; she talked without thinking and without hesitation.

The ultrasound saw through the tissues of my belly, she said. It revealed the child in me, an uncanny thing. And the doctor said: It's going to be a boy. It's going to be a girl. XX or XY was noted down, and the letters made a difference visible only between their legs, the moment they were born. What was the unborn child before that? What stands between girl and boy, between Rico and Leni? What the fuck is this inside me?

Rahel touched the door with one finger, the pale wood.

It felt like there were two bodies in my belly when I was pregnant with Leni, and only one survived. It's Leni, my God, it's my daughter, and I just can't hold her. She's slipping away from me. And so is Boris.

Rahel shifted her weight. The floor creaked beneath her feet, the sound shading this way and that, growing softer, growing louder.

What am I saying? she sighed, and turning she looked first into Fenna's face and then Verena's; both were watching her alertly. Rahel sat down again beside Verena.

I can't remember the moment just after Leni was born when they put her onto my chest, she said. Shit, where's the joy? The feeling of oneness?

Verena slowly stroked Rahel's back, running a hand from her neck to the point just above her tailbone, then planted it back beside her.

What does it mean to you, being a mother? she asked.

A mother is loving, answered Rahel, after a moment's hesitation. Unconditionally.

She smacked her fist – once, twice – against her thigh.

You were never one with that child, said Verena.

Yes I was.

I don't think so. That small heart in a woman's belly starts beating very early. It's not independent of you, of course, but it could have stopped, and you would have lived on. You'll always have to distance yourself from the children.

Rahel stared rigidly at the floor.

It's funny you say that. When you wanted nothing but girls, no boys, she said.

You remember that?

Clearly. Your little hussies.

I was furious. With Erik.

And I missed him, said Rahel. You were always so far away. Unreachable.

You missed it, then, having a traditional family?

We could have used a bit of masculinity.

You mean a man? interjected Fenna.

A paternal figure, Rahel said.

You're sounding a bit last century.

I think a child needs a father too. Squareness, rationality, continued Rahel.

So is Boris that kind of man? asked Fenna.

Rahel was silent for a minute. The floor where she sat was suddenly unendurably hard, and she had to force herself not to stand up.

Again she thumped her fist against her thigh.

It wasn't easy to put up with the other kids talking, she said. One boy in Year Three called me a lesbian, as an insult. I knew the word but I'd never said it out loud. It was a lump of sulphur, yellowish and stinking, and I knew instantly your relationship with Inge wasn't normal. What happened between men and women, on the other hand, I'd already figured out in Year One or Two. I was aware that my vagina was meant for a man. Where did that come from? You lived all that so differently, Verena.

I had no idea you were so preoccupied with these questions, Verena replied. You always seemed so certain.

Oh right, sure, said Rahel. I can still see you in the evenings, like you'd shrunk a few centimetres after work, with those dark circles under your eyes, and when I asked if you ever missed Erik, you looked at me like I was beneath contempt. How was I supposed to confide in you?

Verena was silent for a moment. Then she said: Yes, it was chaos back then. I was working a lot – I didn't have a choice. But it was what it was, even if I am sorry about certain things. We all weave our stories out of experience, and wear them differently.

Now you're taking the easy way out, said Rahel.

Verena looked at her.

What do you need from me today? she asked.

Rahel got to her feet. Outside she saw the apple tree, white blossoms tinged a delicate pink. She opened the window, letting in a warm breeze that lifted and ruffled her hair. Instantly she shut it again. Turning back to Verena and Fenna, she shrugged. Shrugged faster. She broke into a laugh, and for a moment felt free and light, until the heaviness settled again on her chest. Clapping her hand to her mouth, she tried to stifle the sound, but couldn't. She kept laughing, a crude, strident noise that filled the room. Then, controlling herself, she slid to the floor with her back against the wall.

Does it bother you that you're even more tied down now you have a second child? asked Fenna, as though nothing had happened.

Rahel sat unmoving.

Rico and Leni are growing up, she said at last. Their legs are longer, their hands are more dexterous. Soon they'll be walking to kindergarten, and then to school. Meanwhile I'm not going anywhere. I've tried, but no dice. And Boris will leave, I'm sure of it. Sometimes I feel like he's gone already. And me? I still think nearly every day about the day Rico was born, even though it's been more than three years. It's like I'm trapped there, in all those powerful emotions, in the way I felt when I was lying there on the bed. I was in myself and beside myself, and it was right, it was just right. Boris with me, and Rico. Anything seemed possible.

And what about with Leni? asked Fenna.

It's only been five months, but I remember it very differently. Much colder, and like something in me had already tightened up, said Rahel. I'd been having contractions at home, but when I was pacing up and down the hospital corridor they just wouldn't come. Then suddenly I was sitting on this pink exercise ball, rolling my pelvis, something was being inserted, then there was a birthing pool, the contractions started again at last, but the pain was just hammering at me from the outside, and I wanted the fucking epidural right fucking now, but I was stuck waiting forever in this water that was way too warm until the anaesthetist came and jabbed it into my spinal cord, and then the midwife was asking me to push. I tried, I tried to push, but I couldn't feel anything. I just sat there, legs yanked up, chin to breastbone. After what felt like ages, when Leni finally came out, all I saw were her female genitals. That's where my memory cuts off.

As she talked, Rahel's head hung closer and closer to her folded legs, and eventually it drooped completely, so that her forehead was resting on the pointed caps of her knees.

Did you ever talk to anyone about it? asked Verena. To the midwife? Boris?

She raised her head a fraction and shook it slowly.

Boris thinks it's about him. He doesn't get it.

To be honest, said Fenna, I don't get it either.

Rahel sobbed, and the intervals between the sobs grew shorter and shorter, the sounds wrung from deep within, from her throat, chest, belly, groin. Her whole body shook, until suddenly she felt arms that clasped her – mother, sister – and the wall at her back, a warm vessel into which she slid.

You need to get your strength back, said Fenna. Eat something. Apples and cauliflower, beef and leeks, carrots, pasta, cream. And cake.

7

Rahel?

Someone touched her upper arm. Maya wore a green scarf in her hair and bright scarlet lipstick. The colour had rubbed off the inside of her lips, as though she'd just stepped offstage after a long show.

What are you doing here?!

She pulled Rahel to her feet and gave her a quick hug, then put her hands on her shoulders and pushed her away a little.

You look like you've been dragged through a hedge backwards.

Rahel laughed.

Woodland hermit goes on spontaneous holiday, she said, unzipping her rain jacket.

Maya unlocked the door to her flat.

Come in, she said, but don't expect a red carpet.

She chucked her high-heeled boots into a corner and sauntered into the living room. Rahel followed. The décor hadn't changed much since the last time she was there. The bleached purple sofa was in the same corner beside the little table covered in bottles, magazines, cigarette packets and essential oils, and on the floor was the shabby Persian rug. On the wall hung the familiar Montreux Jazz Festival poster from 1984: colourful lettering and a female figure that looked exactly like a Niki de

Saint Phalle, set against a vivid blue background. But the flat was dingier. The plaster was visibly peeling in spots, and the threshold between the hallway and the living room was broken, half snapped away.

They're not doing anything to this place anymore, said Maya, who had noticed Rahel's expression. Whole thing's being torn down. We're out in September. They're putting up a noise barrier along the motorway.

She flopped down onto the sofa and lit a cigarette.

How are you getting on?

She began to massage her toes with her free hand.

Sit down.

Rahel remained standing in front of Maya.

Please, she added.

So, are we working together again? asked Rahel.

Maya stopped massaging.

What do you mean?

I'm back. And we're going to sing.

Yeah, sure, said Maya.

You don't sound enthusiastic.

Well, I mean, you show up here after we haven't been in touch for ages, and suddenly you're in my living room coming out with all this stuff about doing a project together.

Rahel put her hand on Maya's knee and said, Hey bitch. I missed you.

Maya leant forward and hugged Rahel, longer this time.

I've been waiting for this, she said, and gestured towards her pack of cigarettes. Want one?

Rahel shook her head, aware of her swollen, painful breasts.

Back in a minute, she said, and left the room.

She'd already had to pull her top up once today in the train loo, reluctantly putting her hands on each breast and hastily squeezing out some milk. The sink and mirror had ended up spattered with what remained of her existence as a mother. She didn't want to leave any trace in Maya's bathroom, but as she sat on the toilet she tried roughly to disgorge the milk while she emptied her bladder. Nothing happened, no matter how hard she kneaded. In the end she just flushed and went back into the living room.

I'm looking for a studio, said Rahel, sitting next to Maya on the sofa.

Here in Zurich?

Yes.

Are you guys coming back?

No.

Just you?

Yeah.

Did you and Boris split up?

No.

How are the kids?

Are you staying in Zurich? asked Rahel, throwing the question back at her.

You're chatty.

Just tell me!

Maya shook her head, red curls bouncing.

I'm looking for a place in Berlin, starting in the autumn.

Rahel turned to Maya and looked her full in the face. She was getting older: the creases leading from her eyes to the hairline at her temples and on her forehead were deeper than three years ago. Her face seemed to Rahel infinitely beautiful, and she couldn't help putting a finger to the right of Maya's eyelid and tracing the furrows into her hair. Maya smiled.

You're such a funny little wood sprite, she said. I'll grab you something to drink, maybe that'll get you in the mood to talk.

She rose, returning a moment later with two glasses of water.

Can't we just chill for a bit, asked Rahel. Leave all the baggage aside?

Maya clinked her glass with Rahel's.

Sounds perfect, she said. And tonight we're going to Moods, yes? I think you're in need of a decent show.

Definitely, said Rahel.

Maya plugged her phone into the speakers, and out came the voice of Ella Fitzgerald. They listened to 'The Lady Is a Tramp', 'Hello Dolly' and 'Sing Me a Swing Song'. They said nothing but sat on the sofa, their feet tapping towards each other and away. Maya, in her raw-tinged voice, sang along every now and then. Then she typed something into her phone and a New Orleans jazz-style piece began to play; Maya jumped up from the sofa with the words 'Tuba Skinny!' and began to circle her hips.

Come on! she cried, laughing and holding out her arms towards Rahel.

Rahel let herself be hauled to her feet. She danced slowly and tentatively at first, while Maya threw her hands into the air and moved with her whole body, lively and exuberant. Rahel spun around and put the palms of her hands against Maya's;

they giggled like little girls, thought Rahel, like old women. Uplifted.

We should take a bath together, said Rahel. Remember? Like we did before our first show together.

Later, answered Maya. First, a toast. To reuniting!

Rahel sat down on the sofa.

Great. Bring on the buzz!

Maya fetched a bottle of wine and two glasses. She gulped it down, wine like water, set the glass on the table and put her head in Rahel's lap.

Come with me to Berlin, it'll do you good. I met a genius producer. He might be able to do something for you too.

Rahel hadn't answered. Instead she had played with Maya's hair and hummed softly. At some point Maya had fallen asleep, and so there they lay, head in lap, backsides on the sofa, soft fabric, and Rahel had listened to Maya's breathing and the ticking of the clock above the living room door.

8

The carrots they brought up from the cellar felt cool, still caked with particles of soil. The first one Rahel peeled was astonishingly long and bent only at the tip, as though it had suddenly decided to veer off in another direction while it grew. She ran her fingers every now and then over the shining surface, calm and clear, as though she had just washed off a grubby layer of skin. She peeled the rest of the carrots, cut them into thin wafers, and put one into her mouth. Sweet, only a drop of bitterness. Then she took a box of penne from the cupboard and reached inside, the pasta skittering over her hand. Rahel shook half the packet into the salty water. Fenna had cut the caper berries in half and chopped the feta, a large head of broccoli and two kohlrabi into pieces. Setting the cutting board on the counter by the stove, she put a piece of feta in her mouth. The rest of the cheese and the caper berries she scraped into a separate bowl, leaving the vegetables on the board.

Didn't you ever consider a home birth? she asked.

No, said Rahel. Why do you ask?

It didn't sound very nice, what you were saying about the midwives and the doctors.

They were doing their jobs.

Fenna ate another piece of cheese.

I completely get what you were saying earlier about the ultrasound, she said. This probe that sees through you and takes a picture of your baby. Creepy. I don't want to pick and choose. That's why I'm not going to the doctor.

Rahel gave the boiling pasta a stir and turned down the heat a little.

You're not doing any of the checks?

Nope. The stuff they tell you may seem unambiguous at first glance, but that's deceptive.

And what does Luc say about that?

We haven't discussed it yet.

Fenna began to peel an onion.

I mean, there isn't actually anything to discuss.

Rahel looked up from the bubbling saucepan.

If I'm being honest, she said, I do kind of understand where Luc is coming from.

Oh yeah? And what do you know about his opinion, then? asked Fenna.

Why won't you at least take a pregnancy test?

I know myself, for fuck's sake. I'm pregnant. How's some stupid strip of paper supposed to know better than I do? It would say the exact same thing: pregnant! How long have I been monitoring myself, taking pills and regulating my cycle, weighing myself, scanning every pimple? Now I just want to let my body do its thing. Enough already!

Rahel observed her sister's profile. A few strands of hair had come loose and were covering part of her face. Fenna stared at the chopping board in front of her as though she'd forgotten what she was going to do with it.

Has Luc even contacted you yet? asked Rahel.

Fenna turned to Rahel with a surprisingly hard stare. She took the knife from her hand, turned away again and cut the onion into little pieces on a second board, a swift chopping motion.

No.

Well, how did you leave it?

He needs to let this all sink in. It's not easy for him, you know. I mean, he's pretty much the least settled person there is. Heading off from Nepal to Switzerland and back, vegan to carnivore twice a day. And now he's going to be a dad. He needs to process all that.

Think he can handle it? asked Rahel.

Why wouldn't he be able to?

Rahel said nothing.

Anyway, said Fenna, I don't want to get too fixated on him.

Well, that doesn't sound very promising, Rahel said.

In one quick motion, Fenna scraped all the bits of onion into the frying pan. Rahel added a dash of oil and switched on the hob.

So it wasn't a decision you made together, having a child? she asked.

Yes and no. But you know what? We're off topic, Fenna retorted sharply. She went over to the spice rack. Small jars rattled.

So that's a no, then.

He owes me, said Fenna under her breath.

Owes you? Owes you a kid?

I can't explain it to you. Not now.

Just spit it out, you nutter.

Let's talk about it later, OK?

Fenna sat down on a chair and crossed her arms.

You've been putting me off for three days, you know that? said Rahel, adding the chopped vegetables to the pan with the onions.

Yes, I'm aware of that, said Fenna.

She got to her feet.

Can you finish the cooking by yourself? I need fresh air.

9

With a bang louder than Fenna had expected, the front door slammed shut.

Women, she thought furiously, were supposed to have taken back control of their bodies with the invention of the pill and the legalisation of abortion. She gazed at the countryside spread out before her, at the green fields cut through with wooden fences, the hiking trail and the narrow road connecting the two neighbouring farms to Boris and Rahel's house. Apple and pear trees grew at regular intervals between them, and surrounding it all, as though on guard, was the forest. It was all quite nondescript, really. Fenna could have been almost anywhere north of the Swiss Alps or in southern Germany, and yet since Rahel had been living here this eastern Swiss scenery had somehow come to feel specific. The name of the famous French feminist who had written the article about the pill had completely slipped her mind. Reading it a week ago had given Fenna an exalted feeling. She had decided to get pregnant. It was her choice, unlike the women before her.

Fenna took a few steps towards the well, skimmed her hand through the cool water, drew it out and touched her belly, which was growing taut. Truth was, she felt the same as ever – except for this shift outward, as though she were standing a few millimetres away from her own body. In any case, thought

Fenna, flattening a marigold with her foot, it was all much too pretty.

Fenna had starting taking the pill at fourteen, and not long after that she'd had sex for the first time, with a boy four years older whom she'd met at the village youth centre. She'd read that it hurt, your first time, but for her that hadn't been the case.

Guess you're not a virgin anymore, he'd whispered.

Fenna had laughed out loud and answered: I'm a Taurus.

In early puberty she had still pictured the hymen as a wisp of wafer-thin skin stretched across the vagina, which would tear like silk – *rip* – the first time she had sex. There would be blood. Nope, Verena had explained when Fenna asked her. Only teen magazines were obsessed with the hymen. Really it was a collection of ring-shaped mucosal folds also known as a *corona*, Greek for crown or wreath. And this crown, which was unique to women, could not be destroyed by anything or anyone, because it wasn't a purely physical thing.

She would protect that crown forever – ever since her conversation with Verena, that had been one of Fenna's principles. She had taken the pill with a dependability that surprised her, even when she'd been with a girl or was exploring her body alone. She had taken it without thinking about what was in it or what was happening to her body. It wasn't until six months after the incident in the Bosco d'Öss, when it suddenly struck her that she had been deliberately suppressing her ovulation for years, that she thought again about the crown and wondered where it had gone. She made a snap decision to go off the pill, sticking to her guns even when Luc goggled at her after she told him what she'd done.

Don't look so astonished, she said. You're the one who said that artificial hormones would gradually erode my natural femininity.

Luc, for once, didn't answer straight away.

I was more astonished by the timetables telling me when and where we can see each other, he replied at last.

Astonished or annoyed? asked Fenna, sitting next to him on the bed and giving him a tap on the nose.

Luc swatted her hand away.

I'm not massively keen on the idea of a bit of rubber getting between us.

I wish a bit of rubber was all it was.

Sorry?

Forget it, said Fenna.

As far as she was concerned, the contraception issue was settled. From then on she checked her cycle every morning, using a computer program that told her green for no condom, red for definitely condom, and orange for it's a bit dicey. Luc had broached the subject twice, asking whether there were any new contraceptives on the market, and when she hadn't answered he had let it drop.

Inevitably, Fenna's body had changed after she made the switch: suddenly she felt desire stirring for all sorts of things, and the tickling impulse to have a baby. Her mood swings had worsened but overall she'd been more cheerful, which even Luc had noticed. Her breasts were slightly smaller, but also wonderfully soft. Fenna enjoyed touching them, even when she was out and about: she'd slip a hand inside her bra as she crossed at zebra crossings, queued at the supermarket till, stepped into the cool water at the pool. All at once, the breasts that she had never found particularly interesting felt like part of her. She was happy, entirely on her own account.

In a way, it had astounded Fenna what the French feminist had written about the pill and the legalisation of abortion giving women new rights over their bodies. She knew what the woman meant in historical terms; she knew about their significance. But her experience of the pill was different: she couldn't equate the control it had given her with a right. For her, it was the other way around: by coming off the pill she had wrested the power back. She had liberated herself from hormones she had to swallow, hormones that had changed her in ways that in hindsight seemed drastic. She had freed herself from Luc, too, she realised; she had become more independent. She had recovered her crown. Why should she let a doctor examine her body now?

She gave a suppressed burp. She had often wondered where exactly the urge to get pregnant had come from. Where had it crept in – through her nostril or her arsehole or her vagina? She was looking forward to the baby. Not entirely without misgivings, although she didn't want to admit that to Rahel.

Kicking a pebble aside, she walked across the yard and surveyed the house: the brown wooden façade had been subtly coloured by the wind, sun and snow. In the adjoining garden behind the fence were rows of herbs and leeks, salads and a few flowers; a plastic sheet had been pulled over one bed. Two spray bottles were waiting in front of the bushes, one red, one metal.

She'd found it: a place to go, Rahel had told her on the phone a few weeks after meeting Boris. Fenna had roared with laughter and Rahel had been silent for a while.

Do you even know what that means to me? she had asked at last, loudly.

A house, a husband, a son, a daughter, a patch of garden, and now suddenly this emptiness, thought Fenna. And Rahel's crown buried somewhere. Not for me.

Leaning over the fence, she picked a tiny blackberry, green and hard, complete with twig; she felt a slight sting as she clenched her hand into a fist and squeezed. She saw white. Dozens of tablets, small and round, popped into her mouth, summoning life, dispatching life, stirring the blood, bringing sleep, dreams. Fenna closed her eyes. There was a child turning inside her now, yellow limbs rearing, a rift. Fenna looked down at herself – there was nothing. Only the stinging that had been in her palm, and now was multiplied a thousandfold inside her belly.

I O

Last night's dream: a little girl inside me. She'd be pretty, I could see it in the pictures they took. But I knew it wasn't my baby. Someone had put it in my stomach. It pushed down and I felt myself open, making space for the child.

Wake up! Spring. The days are getting longer. The girl is in my lap, opening and closing her eyes, licking her fingers like sweets.

They ate a late lunch, vegetables with pasta, cheese and beef; Rahel opened a bottle of wine, poured herself a glass and put the cork back in the bottle. Verena pushed her food around on her plate, taking a long time to chew each bite. She asked Rahel to open the window. Pulling out a handkerchief, she wiped beads of sweat from her forehead.

I'm cold at night and hot during the day, she said, shrugging. Side effect of the chemo.

She got quieter and quieter until at some point she excused herself to Fenna and Rahel, saying she wasn't feeling well and had to lie down. Would they come up and see her later?

Both nodded.

They were silent a long time as they washed up; Rahel was busy in the foamy water, Fenna with the checked tea towel. Rahel was careful to let the questions she wanted to ask her sister burst like bubbles on the water. Questions about Luc, about the pregnancy, about the child.

Once the dishes were washed and dried, they went outside to sit on the deckchairs behind the house. By now the sky had cleared and the sun was dazzling. The meadows shimmered yellow with the marigolds. Rahel had brought the breast pump, and she opened her short-sleeved blouse, button by button, undid the left side of the nursing bra, positioned the funnel and began to pump by hand. There was a mechanical, rhythmic sound. After thirty seconds the milk came through, dripping into the funnel.

I'm a dairy cow, Rahel sneered without looking up.

Will we be using it to make rice pudding later? asked Fenna, flicking a few dandelion seeds off the top of her deckchair.

Ugh, that would gross me out, Rahel said.

Have you ever tried it?

I haven't, but Rico still loves it.

You still breastfeed him?

I give him some of the milk I pump.

You really don't want to cut the apron strings.

As long as he likes it, why not?

Fenna leant back in her deckchair. Rahel pumped insistently; she had already collected a few centilitres.

My milk is meant for Leni, she said. Cow's milk for a calf. But it makes a lot more sense giving Rico mine than a cow's.

Fenna laughed.

Do you want more kids, you and Boris?

Rahel was quiet for a minute. Then she said: I don't think so.

Two's not bad, said Fenna. Verena definitely couldn't have handled any more than two.

Did she say that?

Not exactly.

Rahel removed the pouch of milk, held it up and briefly examined the white liquid. Then she poured the contents into the flowerpot beside her deckchair.

What a waste! exclaimed Fenna.

The flowers are happy, countered Rahel. And anyway, I'm weaning them. Finally.

She did up the left side of the nursing bra and undid the right, then adjusted the pump.

I barely recognise Verena, she said. It's like the cancer has gnawed away at her old brusqueness.

I know what you mean, said Fenna. But she hasn't been as blunt as she used to be for ages, not since the diagnosis.

Fenna tipped her zebra-patterned sunglasses off her temples onto her nose, her eyes vanishing behind the dark lenses.

You didn't ever want a daughter, did you? she asked.

The sound of the pump broke off. A drop of milk had escaped the funnel and was trickling towards Rahel's belly button; with a quick sweep of her hand she brushed it away. Then she began to pump again.

Nonsense, she said.

What stands between Rico and Leni, between girl and boy? said Fenna. It's been on your mind, you said so yourself.

Rahel looked down at her stomach. The drop of milk had left a gleaming film.

Do you remember how Mum used to say the word cunt sometimes? Fenna went on. To wash your cunt you don't need soap, just water. Your cunt is where the baby comes out, and so on. And because of her I thought it was a normal word. Until we had sex ed at school. I still remember us standing around the classroom table in Year Six, giggling, and Tobler presenting this tiny little diagram of a penis and vagina.

Tobler in his final throes as a teacher? asked Rahel.

Yeah, he retired not long after that. I didn't say anything as he explained that there were correct names for female genitalia and incorrect ones. The incorrect ones were cunt, pussy and gash. Can you imagine how quietly he said the words and how crumpled he looked? I was gobsmacked, and on the way home after that absurd sex ed class I kept muttering the word to myself: I love my cunt, I stroke my cunt. And you know what? In that book Verena gave you the other day, *Vulva*, it says that cunt comes from Old English, and the original meaning is 'sacred place'. Cunt is related to queen, country and kin.

Rahel blinked at Fenna.

Are you saying Verena knew that?

Fenna shrugged.

You know her. She's a house of a hundred rooms.

Hundred and fifty, at least, said Rahel.

She was silent a while before she went on. Sometimes I wonder what Verena was like before Erik left. In the photos with him she looks so different, but I barely remember those days.

They could hear birds chirping nervously. A woman was hiking along the footpath. Her dog made a dash towards Fenna and Rahel, tongue lolling, but the woman gave a piercing whistle and the animal turned back at once, trotting obediently a few metres behind its mistress.

Rahel removed the pump, set it on the ground and shook the contents of the pouch into the grass.

Does Verena like being here? she asked.

Don't you worry your pretty little head about that, Fenna said. It's always been like this. Whenever she's at the start of a holiday or somewhere unfamiliar, boom, Mum gets tired and sleeps all day. She needs time.

You know, said Rahel, you were the right daughter for Verena. Something I could never have been.

Ah, give over.

I was too weak, too quiet. Erik didn't know what to do with me, and neither did Verena.

Fenna shook her head vigorously, as Rahel got heavily to her feet.

I'm melting in this awful heat, she said. I need a minute to myself.

Now that I understand, said Fenna.

For weeks Rahel had been drawn to the hide nearly every day, always early in the morning. She had never set off as late as she did that day. The place was already much too busy, the sun too strong, the clearing below too bright. Just as she was opening her notebook, she heard a group of hikers tramp past behind the hide. Loud voices. She didn't move a muscle, but felt caught out nonetheless. What if a hunter comes along? she wondered for the umpteenth time. How would she explain her presence there, in a place that was never meant for her? I'm doing my homework? This home is where I work. My work *is* this home?

Rahel opened and closed the notebook several times. The questioning, ever-probing, stifling feeling she got when she thought about Leni was abruptly far away, just like Leni herself, and what she had written about Boris, about that dream, seemed ridiculous. He had never accused her of neglecting the housework, he had never made fun of her appearance. And an aluminium bath, what was that all about? She leafed through her notebook, hoping to jog her memory about when she'd had that dream. But the memory wouldn't come, so she picked up her pen and resolved to describe the pine trees around her, big and small, and the noises of the forest. It was impossible. She didn't write a single word, but the talk she'd had with Boris before the dream popped back into her head.

Do you not see that by rejecting Leni you're rejecting me too? he had asked, after she turned down his offer to take the kids out for the day.

When she asked Boris what he meant by that, he'd explained: You adore Rico and you reject Leni. Your child. And my child. Do you really not see what I mean?

Rahel had shaken her head vehemently and said: You're letting your imagination run away with you.

And why do you only fuck me because you think it keeps me happy? he had pressed on angrily. Why do you ignore my presence and everything I do? You've only got eyes for yourself and Rico, and you hold Leni like she's some sort of fucking duty!

Rahel had stood up from the table.

You have no idea what it feels like to give birth to a child, she had responded soberly.

And he had loudly retorted: And you have no idea what it feels like when you treat me this way.

The wind set the pines swaying. Rahel's breath rattled. Taking up the pen once more, she wrote a few thematically coherent words: *tectonic*, *limestone*, *clearing*. It seemed as though Boris's words were only just reaching her now, days after the fact. Again there was that sting in her chest, around her lips.

What if he doesn't come back? she thought, swallowing tears. She would have liked to tell him something, but didn't know exactly what. Perhaps that even she didn't understand what had happened in Zurich, and had no idea how to find words for it. And that she was gradually beginning to understand what he had meant about Leni and him.

Rahel erased what she had written, started afresh, and all at once she felt a tug, an undertow in which the rest was forgotten, in which she arranged word after word, fusing them into a whole, into a text. Immediately she re-read the lines and tried to sing the lyrics; the naked words were elevated by the handful of notes, by a simple melody.

Her footsteps tentative but lighter, Rahel went back home to Verena and Fenna. The three of them spent the rest of the afternoon and evening in one room, together but keeping to themselves, for the most part silent, reading, Verena eventually nodding off, as a hush settled over Fenna and Rahel as well.

Just before eight, Verena suddenly looked up from the sofa, wide awake, and said loudly: Today is Mother's Day!

She lay back down. Fenna and Rahel heard her soft laughter, then minutes later her slow breath.

They went upstairs early. Rahel stretched out in her bed. Silence. No sighs, no breath, no burbling baby. She picked up her phone and typed a message to Boris.

How's it going?

Then she slowly deleted every single letter and switched off her phone. How quickly you get used to someone's presence, she thought as the screen went black, how quickly to their absence. She turned from one side to the other side and back again. At last she ended up on her back. Tomorrow, she said to herself, tomorrow I'll dig my hands into the earth. She shut her eyes and her mind wandered again to Rico's birth, to the way she had opened, and she fell asleep before the child she was imagining had even left her body. She fell asleep with its head inside her birth canal.

12

They took the tram to Hardbrücke. Rahel hadn't told Maya anything about the pain in her breasts, which had intensified the longer they sat on the sofa. A tussle in Rahel's body: every sip of wine dulled the pain, but the moment she stopped drinking for a minute or two, it regained the upper hand.

They had put off taking a bath together until the next day, and Rahel hadn't said much about what was going on in her life. Maya was far less reticent about her tours and her plans for Berlin. They had reminisced about old times: about the gig when Maya got so drunk that Rahel, who had been sitting in the audience, replaced her on vocals after the interval; about nocturnal skinny-dipping in the river and forbidden jam sessions on the roof of the building where Chris had lived. Meanwhile Rahel kept trying to stroke the milk out of her breasts in the bathroom, but not a drop came out. Her breasts felt like two glowing stones. She pushed the thoughts of Boris, Rico and Leni that came crowding into that one and a half by two metre space towards the border between the wall and the ceiling. Staggering back into the living room, where Maya had just shoved a piece of ham toastie into her mouth, she said: Alright, off to Moods!

They walked past Zurich's biggest carwash, leaving a racket of cars and trams behind them, then arrived at the Schiffbau: a brick building, the windows tall and narrow. Outside there were already throngs of people, chatter and loud laughter; two guys pulled up on bikes, wearing hipster beanies like the young man that morning on the train. Rahel closed her eyes and soaked in the mix of voices, rushing cars, beeping, wind, squealing trams and Maya's shoes clacking on the tarmac; the background noise maintained a comfortable distance, as though she were swaddled in an insulating blanket. Hooking an arm through hers, Maya dragged her towards the entrance. Her friend Lennard was playing today, she said. He'd put both their names on the guest list. Rahel plodded along in echo of Maya's rhythm.

That afternoon they'd downed a bottle and a half of wine, plus shots. The alcohol had soon mixed pleasantly with Rahel's blood, and she kept bouncing up and down. Electro jazz.

Lennard was Austrian, Maya had met him at a concert in Vienna, and for nearly a year they'd been in a relationship with three vertices: Vienna, Zurich, Berlin.

He fucks like Adam, Maya had said back at the flat, giggling happily.

And that means?

Divinely. I could come on the spot every single time.

Rahel had laughed and thought briefly of Eve and A., the image she had pasted together: the feminine face of Dürer's painted Adam, which she had glued next to Eve's body.

Seriously, Maya had said, clicking the black-varnished nail of her right index finger against her empty glass.

And he plays like he fucks, she added. Then, getting to her feet, she said: I'll see if I've got any more wine.

They stepped into the large foyer. It was hot, with the scent of wax in the air. A group of elegantly dressed people were toasting something with glasses of Prosecco, while beside them a woman swung her green dreadlocks over her shoulder. Nothing had changed since Rahel's last visit: there they still were, the sixty-year-old women with short dyed-black hair and thick-rimmed glasses, rubbing shoulders with younger people in checked jackets and knitwear. The whole colourful mix. A man in a suit sauntered across the double-height room and set his wine glass on a table; at the bar, two young women were deep in conversation: unkempt, leather jackets, mid-calf boots. Rahel had stuffed her tracksuit bottoms and woolly jumper into her rucksack with the rain jacket, leaving it in Maya's bedroom. She had raided Maya's wardrobe and chosen black, slightly see-through leggings, a burgundy miniskirt and a silk blouse in traffic-light red. Over it she wore a lightweight brown coat and black bag. The clothes were a size too big, and every few feet she had to pull the blouse down a little and the skirt up a little, but she liked the smell of Maya's washing powder and the sense of wearing a new velvety skin. All she wore of her own were her trainers, which were still clumped with mud from the forest. For the first time in a long while, she felt infinitely light and calm. Just stay here, she thought, as she sat down on a barstool and Maya placed a glass of Campari and orange in front of her.

13

Rahel woke to the sound of a dull knock and the door squeaking, soft footsteps on the wooden floor, then a hand groping towards her.

It's me, said Fenna.

She got in next to Rahel and pulled up the duvet on Boris's side of the bed.

I had an awful dream.

Rahel said nothing. The night weighed heavily on her.

Tell me, she said at last.

I met Luc in the middle of an oval meadow surrounded by dark trees, began Fenna in a soft voice. We took off our clothes, piece by piece, and the meadow transformed into a lake. We swam in circles around each another. Luc's dark eyes changed, they grew bigger and bigger, he stared at me, and I knew that underneath his skin there was something else. That something was churning there. We pushed each other's heads under the surface of the water, and when I dived down I saw water lilies, then tulips too, daisies, marigolds. We didn't let go, the water was swirling, and suddenly his skin was sloughing off in ribbons, it came towards me in the water, and beneath it was a second skin, burned black but still glowing with heat, and it stank. Then I woke up. Luc's insides are decaying, I thought. And I was sure I could save him with the picture I had of him in my head. I know now one of the reasons why I'm still with him. I feel sorry for him.

Rahel was instantly wide awake.

What for?

He's so lost in this world he's just sort of patched together for himself. Fundamentally he's a good person, he just doesn't have any perspective, you know. He hurt me once when we were hiking, and I only realised afterwards that it happened because of all the lostness in him that had built up.

I don't understand a single word you're saying, Fenna. What did he do?

He wanted me, I mean, he had me, in the forest. I hated him at first, after he did that, but then I understood. That I had been sending signals. I wanted him to let me in, otherwise I wouldn't have gone that far. I mean, yes, I bought the whole open relationship thing at first, and in a way I even enjoyed it, and I put up with his moods, his comings and goings. I did that because I wanted him close to me, so close we could stand nose to nose and genuinely know each other. I wanted synthesis.

Fenna paused.

I was naïve, she went on. It couldn't have led to anything except what Luc did.

He forced you to have sex?

I thought so at first. Then I realised I wanted it too.

But he was rough with you?

Because of him, I understood something. Our respective weaknesses. I had subjugated myself to him and didn't notice.

She took another breath.

He took what he needed. And now I've done the same. That's why I got pregnant.

What the hell is wrong with you?! gasped Rahel.

I'll take good care of the baby, and Luc is bound to be in touch soon.

Rahel tried to make out Fenna's expression, but it was too dark.

Have you ever heard of Heba? asked Fenna, still almost in a whisper. That's what they called Eve in pre-Israelite mythology. The earth goddess. Abdiheba, her servant, became Adam in the Bible. But the story in pre-Israelite mythology is different from the one we know. I saw the picture that was on the floor in the hallway the other day, the one of Eve and Adam's head. Is that yours?

Without stopping for an answer, she went on.

Anyway, Heba gave Abdiheba the apple, which didn't just represent love but also death. He ate it, meaning he was united with her through sex, and he died. So Heba gave him eternal life and eternal youth in the paradise of the apple trees.

Fenna giggled.

Although I'd have preferred the paradise of figs, she added. Fig comes from the ancient Greek *fica*, and *fica* is another term for vulva.

Where are you going with this? asked Rahel.

In the Bible the story goes like this: Eve and Adam are already in paradise when they eat the apple. They're subsequently banished and eventually die, because they've lost eternal life. To enjoy the apple, or the fig, is to do something supposedly wicked. It's a sin. And the woman is the origin of that sin. All in all, Eve has a very definite and reduced place in the Bible. She was created from Adam's rib, so from him. Abdiheba, on the other hand, can only stay in paradise because Heba allows him to. Because *she* gives him the apple. Because *she* has created him.

Yes, and?

By now Rahel's eyes were more accustomed to the darkness. She could make out details, Fenna's face, mask-like, the tip of her nose moving faintly back and forth as she spoke.

Luc was also trying to do something to me that I didn't get at first. He also wanted to get inside me. He thought maybe he could reach some kind of paradise that way. But I have the key, I'm the one who opens it. Or allows it. I allowed what he did to me, but he didn't really get to me. I've realised that. Where he wanted to go there's a baby growing now. Something new is coming – between him and me, too.

Fenna, said Rahel, you're loopier than ever.

Don't you get it?

What exactly am I supposed to get? Luc hurt you, and you're trying to downplay it!

You're not seeing the bigger picture.

That you're pregnant. What's going to happen now, then?

Luc will come, I know that.

What are you using this baby for?

Fenna was very close to Rahel now. There was astonishment in her wide eyes.

How can you ask something like that?!

You make it sound like you need it for something, said Rahel, cutting her off.

Isn't the decision to have a child always selfish, when it comes down to it? And the exact opposite at the same time? asked Fenna.

Normally it's not that calculating.

Fenna shook her head fervently.

Anyway, Luc hasn't realised yet that it's up to me whether he can stay. He still sees himself as a man who takes what he wants and keeps his dagger in his wife's sheath, as though he could own her.

Sounds a bit unilateral, said Rahel. So does your version of living together, though.

There are things I give him, and obviously things he gives me as well. Give and take – you know, usual story. But there's something to it.

Is there anything else keeping you in the relationship? asked Rahel.

I love him, Fenna said without hesitation. His fundamental nature. And lots of stuff to do with the way he looks at things. The way he challenges me.

She struck the flat of her hand several times against her breastbone.

You know how hard it is to explain, she went on. But it's about finding a new version. One where both of us take what we need. One where both of us respect our boundaries. For far too long I didn't understand what that meant. I don't want a house with him, he doesn't have to promise me that he'll be faithful in the traditional sense, only that he's honest with me and shows me every aspect of himself. What I'm picturing is a dynamic kind of love, one with space for all the stuff below the surface.

And in this version you're independent of him? asked Rahel.

Yes.

Don't take this the wrong way, but do you really think this theory is any less naïve than the one you had before?

Fenna turned away without answering.

I'm finding it harder than I thought not to smoke.

You know, said Rahel, raising a child is not as simple as you might think. You need a degree of stability. You'll find yourself reaching limits you can't even imagine right now. And you'll have to rely on Luc.

Rahel touched Fenna's shoulder.

Why don't we go and have some warm milk? she said.

Getting no response, she bent over her sister. Fenna was asleep.

Rahel peeled back the duvet, got up and felt her way over to the bedroom door, along the dark corridor and down the stairs; the glare from the fridge hurt her eyes. She poured some milk into a pan, switched on the hob, spooned some honey into a cup, tipped in the milk and stirred.

Rahel crept into Fenna's room. There on the floor, beside the mattress, lay *Vulva*. Sipping gingerly at the milk and honey, she opened the book. Then she went back to her room, reading, and lay down next to Fenna again. After the fourth sentence, she fell asleep.

14

Stamps on their wrists, into Moods, reddish light made denser by the ruby velvet curtains along the right-hand side of the room, candles on the little tables. They sat down. Maya looked Rahel up and down.

You look good, she said.

Ready for the stage, eh?

Just got to get rid of those shoes, Maya retorted.

They make the outfit unique.

Ridiculous, more like.

Rahel's eyes flitted to her grimy trainers, then wandered across the room. Already many of the tables were occupied, most by people fiddling with their phones. How many times had Boris tried to reach her that day? Once, ten times, a hundred? Rahel took a sip from her glass. She'd rather not know.

To be honest, Rahel, I could never really see you as a mum, Maya began out of nowhere. I mean, there's so much you could do with yourself and your voice, and instead you go and hole up by a hearth in the woods. Nothing against kids, genuinely, and yours are definitely super cute. But still, this right here – I mean, come on.

Maya threw up her arms and immediately let them drop.

And just so you know, I was really upset when you ghosted me.

Rahel turned the stem of the glass full circle in her fingers, as the thought of Leni's outstretched arms flashed across her mind. She downed her drink.

Well I'm here now, she said.

Did you come for a night? A week? Just showing up in Zurich in a woolly jumper?

Ah, you know me.

Maya opened her lips as though to say something, but at that moment the house lights dimmed and the musicians walked onstage. The drummer wore a navy peaked cap, while the rest of the band had artfully messy hair. After a burst of applause, Lennard began to play. Quietly at first, urgently, then ever louder and more virtuosic, just him and his drums. As the tempo reached its peak, the trumpets and a high female voice joined in. It took Rahel a moment to wrench her eyes off the drumsticks in Lennard's hands before she too was swept along by the music's carefree nonchalance. They were on a whole new level, these sounds, and Rahel shivered. She was here, she was back, and she raised her arms to fly while Maya swayed beside her. In the third piece the pianist introduced new accents, bringing a touch of melancholy into the room, which at first seemed to clash but then brought everything along with it: the vocals, the trumpet, the bass, the drums, the audience. The light changed from red to violet. Fractures appeared, between the clear vocals and a kind of guttural rap. Both styles felt absolutely authentic, yet with each change it seemed to Rahel as though the freckle-faced, full-lipped person in front of her were split in half, as though there were two singers onstage, and one was too many. After each final chord, Rahel wished the urgency, the brightness would come back, but the music pushed on, tumbling into the deep, until the vocals were merely high, jarring notes: Gimme – gimme – gimme – gimme – gimme – your – gimme – your – love – gimme – gimme – your – love – gimme – your; then abruptly all Rahel could see was Leni, unshakeable, her round baby's face, her mouth ajar, her tongue clearly visible on the roof of her mouth, and she felt so infinitely sorry for the girl, so buried under all those notes. Rahel jumped and looked at Maya. Her pointed noise, flat cheeks and bouncy hair shone in the light. Rahel put her hand on her shoulder, bent forwards and pulled her close. Then she pressed her lips to Maya's, darted her tongue into her mouth, and there it was, its counterpart, a prancing tongue, leaping like an animal; they were one. A throbbing began in the core of Rahel's chest, carrying to her nipples and through them, and everything felt simultaneously wet and heavy and beautiful; Maya pushed her away and stared, eyelids quivering. Rahel looked down. Two dark circles had appeared on the traffic-light red fabric of the blouse. Grabbing her jacket, she held it protectively in front of her body.

Cigarette! said Rahel.

What?

Maya's face was still so close, anger in it and amazement.

Outside? stammered Rahel.

No, I'm staying here, Maya answered, turning back towards the stage.

Rahel hurried through the darkened space as though being sucked through the hose of a vacuum cleaner, through the violet light, past the heavy red curtains and the bar, through the high main door. Outside the club she found herself staring at the luminous spiral staircase that led up to Hardbrücke Bridge. Her mind raced up, step by step; she pressed on, hunched and swift, under the bridge and towards the station, on, just on, she thought, entering the underpass that led to the platforms. She wanted to be gone. She had to go back.

I 5

Rahel gave a start. The arm she could feel was too long for Rico's, the back too broad. Opening her eyes, she saw her sister's fair hair spread out across the pillow. Fenna, lying next to her. Rahel rubbed a hand across her face, where tiny clumps of sleep had formed in the corners of her eyes. She was very thirsty. Half-buried under her pillow was the book about the vulva. Now she remembered last night's conversation. Fenna twitched.

What am I doing here? she asked.

You didn't sleep well, Rahel said, so you came in here.

What did I say?

You told me about a dream. About Luc. Something about Eve and mythology.

Whatever it was, said Fenna, forget it.

Why should I?

Fenna hitched the duvet up over her head.

My stomach hurts. Leave me alone, she said, sounding muffled.

Do you want anything to drink?

When she didn't respond, Rahel went on: Look, just tell me, what did Luc do to you?

Nothing.

Fenna, I don't recognise you like this!

I'd like a coffee, said Fenna, pulling the covers down off her face as though in slow motion.

As Rahel stood waiting in the kitchen for the coffee to brew, she downed half a litre of water in one go and ate a slice of white bread. She thought briefly of Maya reaching for the last bit of ham toastie in her Zurich apartment, examining it briefly then popping it into her mouth. She could still remember the taste of her tongue, as though she'd kissed her only a minute ago, slightly salty; a taste of the old days.

When Rahel came back into the room, Fenna was lying in exactly the same position as before. Her skin looked waxy. Sitting down on the edge of the bed, Rahel passed her the coffee and put the water on the nightstand. Fenna set the cup next to the water without taking a sip.

What you said last night about staying with Luc because you feel sorry for him, I just don't get it, Rahel began.

You misunderstood, Fenna said immediately.

What's to misunderstand?

Fenna clicked her tongue, as though obviously this was a question Rahel could answer for herself.

Then: It's about the way we see our roles, she said. The roles we're stuck in. Luc, and me as well. I feel sorry for him because he can't get beyond this masculine role he's playing. And me, I'm the one who instigated the whole thing, because I guess I had to learn something from it.

You're rationalising the situation because you can't bring yourself to leave him, said Rahel.

No, I'm facing up to it.

You wanted something from him that he can't give you. That's life.

Rahel lifted her feet off the floor and splayed her bare toes.

Did he hit you? she asked, letting her feet slap back onto the ground.

Fenna bored her fist into the duvet.

Jesus, no, he didn't. We had pretty standard sex, I told you.

But he was rough. What makes you so sure it won't happen again?

Have you even been listening? asked Fenna. I *told* you it was partly me, as well. Anyway, I assume you don't believe he's inherently violent. Biologically, I mean.

He wasn't born that way, if that's what you're saying.

Exactly.

But what kind of relationship is it going to be, if this is what it's based on?

Rahel, there's no point discussing it any further. Just trust me. And now, said Fenna, turning to the wall, I'd like you to leave me in peace.

You realise you're in my bed? Rahel protested.

I'll be out of here in a minute.

Fenna didn't move a muscle as Rahel walked around the bed, sat down and looked directly into her face. She didn't look great – puffy, like she'd been out at some crazy party all night.

You're probably right that I don't understand the first thing about your view of relationships, she said, a little more gently.

Fenna darted out a hand, clutched the mug of coffee and drank greedily.

We're coming from very different places. It's not exactly news, she said, clomping the mug down.

Come on, my little tearaway. It's just never enough for you, is it? said Rahel, her voice wavering between irony and anger. Come on, up we get.

She tugged at the duvet, bringing it sailing to the floor. Fenna wore a pale-yellow tank top. Her left breast was half exposed and her soft belly revealed, the navel bulging in the middle.

Fenna giggled and stared at her, unabashed.

A little tearaway in *your* bed.

Rahel sat back down.

Do you think your perception of men would be different if you hadn't grown up in an all-female household? she asked.

Stupid question. Take a good look at yourself.

Fenna prodded her waist with her foot.

The only real difference between you and me is that I wish I'd had a dad, said Rahel. More than you, anyway.

You're loyal, that's another difference, added Fenna. You're faithful and sincere. And capable of maintaining a healthy distance.

She paused.

At least, you used to be.

Rahel was silent. She felt caught out, like at the hide the day before. Enfolding Fenna's foot in both hands, she pushed it away.

This whole time I thought I didn't need singing anymore, she said. I dropped it straight away, when I first got pregnant with Rico. Then recently I tried to go back. But the only thing

I got from seeing Maya in Zurich, after I'd literally just had Leni glued to my miserable chest, is the realisation that it's not that easy. I was looking to find something I'd lost, but that's only possible *with* Leni.

Rahel brushed Fenna's heel with her palm.

I've always thought that, more than anything else, singing and writing was about letting go and saying goodbye. Distancing yourself. Like in those old songs about Erik. But it's more than that. It's a way of starting afresh, too. Moving on. I couldn't write a thing until the day after you showed up here.

Song lyrics? asked Fenna.

Not really. Just everyday stuff. I've got no choice but to start with the basics and hopefully use the words for songs later on.

Basic stuff or banal stuff? Are you writing about the house, the kitchen, the washing up?

More about Leni.

Then I take back the 'banal' bit.

Well, a daughter's not really anything special, said Rahel.

You can't seriously be saying that.

She demands too much of me, Rahel said.

Because she's a girl? asked Fenna.

I want something else for Leni. Only the best, though.

Then you've got to look after *yourself* first!

If only it was that easy.

Fenna ran her fingers over her belly, tracing from the hem of her shirt to the band of her underwear; her fingernails left bright red marks on the skin.

Do you ever let loose a bit in your lyrics? asked Fenna.

Rahel gave her a quizzical look.

You know, do you ever do anything a bit outrageous in them?

What do you mean?

Well, like, do you ever cheat on Boris in them, or something?

After a brief hesitation, Rahel laughed out loud and said: Sometimes I make a dildo out of paper. Well, a dildo out of stories, actually. It really is the next best thing to good sex, believe me. Experiencing something, freeing myself through writing. Yeah, I do that.

And that's enough for you? asked Fenna. A one-night stand with words?

Rahel laughed.

Well, that's getting older for you, little sister.

You're sounding geriatric.

I'm getting there.

Fuck's sake, you're not even thirty-one! said Fenna. Have you really never had the urge to be with anyone except Boris in the last couple of years? I don't just mean physically. At least take a few days for yourself, spend time with other people instead of playing nursemaid around here?

Rahel's forehead had taken on a slight sheen. She said: I just need to write more, I'll be fine then. I need to slowly get back to singing. It will bring me closer to Leni, too.

To me it sounds more like you're scared, said Fenna. Scared that it will all slip through your fingers if it's not right in front of you.

Fenna pulled her shirt down a little.

By the way. Before, when I said a healthy distance, I meant something different, she added. You're not living at a healthy distance from your family, or healthily close. The longer I've been here, the more I've felt like we need two totally different things, you and me. I need boundaries. And you need to finally open up.

Rahel jumped to her feet.

If you weren't pregnant I'd get you a beer right now, she said. I need a drink.

Then get one.

There was a subdued knock at the bedroom door.

Rahel?

It opened to reveal Verena in the doorway. She seemed remarkably wide awake.

Have you already had breakfast? she asked. I'm starving.

16

I think words: limestone, sediment, folding. Magmatic pressure, primal earth, rugged landscape, karst. I imagine that this is the ground on which I stand, a ground made of words from books; cave landscapes, subterranean passageways. Tectonic shivers beneath the skin.

It seems simpler, what I see now: spruces, firs, beeches. I hear birds, dozens of voices I cannot distinguish, cannot name. A place of grass below me, which makes no sense as yet. A clearing. That's what they call it.

17

The meadow was a fierce green, a plane of orange, yellow, violet and white daubs that carried on uphill, and beyond it was the blue sky, small clouds unhurriedly changing shape, coalescing, separating. They walked at a leisurely pace, as though in a museum: Fenna, Verena, Rahel.

Let's try not to step on any flowers, Fenna had suggested as they set out, and only Rahel had laughingly agreed. Verena had buttoned her light coat to the top; the pale-yellow linen fell to her hips, and her hands in the wide sleeves were small. She wore loose olive-green trousers that she no longer filled out: gospel-style robes, thought Rahel, that billowed in the wind and would one day sweep Verena away. She walked mutely beside them.

Rahel kept hearing a chaffinch chirping the same tune. Her footsteps in the grass were firm, although she took her time over the path, more time than she had ever taken alone. She had often walked this way in recent years: through tall late-spring grass, over freshly cut fields and in the warm, dry wind, when she felt as though her skin might tear away, in the golden autumn, in the fog, through snow or slush that squelched underfoot. She had trodden this way with a child, with two children, with Boris and without, the same route, mostly, and never got bored, far from it; it was soothing to be always passing the same things:

past the pear tree with the crooked branch, past the dark fence and past the well that had long since run dry, outside the disused barn by the wayside.

I never told you about Erik's letter, said Rahel, taking herself by surprise.

What letter? asked Verena.

He wrote to me nearly ten years ago, when I was still a student, shortly after my first album was released.

Fenna, walking ahead of them, whirled around.

You secretive little weasel, she said in a hard voice, but her expression was amused.

What did it say? asked Verena. Drawing level with Fenna, she put her hand on her daughter's back and pushed gently. Fenna started moving again.

Rahel took a deep breath.

He said I had a nasty personality. And he had some disparaging things to say about my songs.

That's all? asked Fenna.

She nodded.

That's a shitty way to say a belated goodbye.

So was mine.

What, just because you sang a few songs about a deadbeat dad?

I ripped him to shreds.

Rightly so, said Fenna, stamping her foot. Why didn't you tell me? We could have gone to see him together and confronted him!

I wanted to deal with it in my own way. And I was ashamed. Of my frankness. The way I'd exposed myself. Suddenly, the songs sounded perverse to my ears too.

Rubbish, said Fenna. You're telling stories in those songs, they're not about an actual father.

Verena cleared her throat.

He's just got old and grumpy, I suppose, she said.

Old, definitely, said Fenna. He must be about sixty-five by now. And bald.

A plane rumbled overhead, and for a moment Rahel thought she felt the earth vibrate. Grabbing onto Verena for support, she righted herself again.

His hair used to be lovely, said Verena, touching the edge of Fenna's. Fair and curly, like yours.

She let her arm drop back to her side. They walked on in silence, Rahel pulling off her thin sweater and tying it round her hips.

The thing I've been wondering for ages, said Rahel, is whether Erik actually wanted kids in the first place?

It was a joint decision.

But he didn't want girls, said Rahel, knotting the sleeves of the jumper a second time. Why?

I don't know what you mean, Verena said.

That's what you said back then, persisted Rahel. That he didn't want girls. Women.

No, that's not right.

Rahel looked from Verena to the field and back again, her head flicking back and forth, her vision green and yellow, the landscape swirling. Her hands dangled by her sides like two weights.

After I got that letter, Rahel went on after a while, for a long time I couldn't write at all. My hand got clumsy and heavy, I couldn't hold a pen, but I was singing all the time. My style

changed overnight, from straight down the line to free, impro-
vised jazz that basically no one wanted to hear, because it was
loud and there were no words. And suddenly I couldn't stand
Chris anymore. I felt sick at the sight of him.

She paused, then added softly: The way the sight of Boris
makes me sick now, sometimes. Only fleetingly. But it's
noticeable.

They reached a fence and followed the track alongside it,
past straggling nettles. After a while, they came across a patch
of marsh where other plants grew, wild orchids, yellow irises,
docks and downy birches, their slim trunks glimmering redly.

Verena came to a halt.

I had no idea there was a marsh up here! she said, bending
down to look at a pink flower.

Fenna leant against the fence.

Rahel turned to look back up the way they'd come. An
image of Chris had snagged in her brain: his smile. She had
broken up with him shortly after Erik's letter, but could hardly
believe it even at the time. She had told him his very presence
was holding her back, that she had to try something new, and
no, he hadn't done anything wrong, he was a great guy, and no,
that wasn't reason enough to stay with him; yes, she was sure,
she couldn't do it anymore, not another night. Even so, they
had slept together one last time. She had grabbed hold of him
roughly, and with eyes closed he had let her do it. Afterwards
she had pulled away from him immediately, held out his clothes
and told him to leave. It was over.

She'd never have thought it possible that they would be a
couple again five years later, albeit only for a few months. In

the intervening years, when they'd both been studying jazz at the same college, they had crossed paths often. Whenever they bumped into each other he had been reserved, but occasionally he would send a text to say he missed her, missed their conversations, her shoulder blades beneath his hands, her scent. It wasn't until they left college that she got involved with him a second time. She'd listened to 'Daddy Longleg' with him once again, falling back into the way she'd felt when she was trying to describe her father and say her goodbye. But she couldn't help it: Chris was too good for her and he wanted her too much. She left him after a couple of weeks, after the affair began with Martin. Chris sent her Dürer's Eve when he found out, and there were no more texts.

Rahel bent down towards her mother.

Marsh orchid, said Verena, pointing at the flower in front of her.

They looked like hanging folds of skin, the slender, pink-and-white blossoms, juicy and soft. She saw Chris and saw her father in her mind's eye, two images superimposed that slowly mingled and volatilised, leaving a leisurely pulse deep inside.

Tell me about Erik, Verena, she said, rising. It sounds like you've softened towards him.

Leaving the boggy field, they walked on, towards more forest that unstretched before their feet.

What do you want to know? asked Verena.

How you met, Rahel said. And what happened between you.

Verena fixed her eyes on the ground, and a moment passed before she began to speak.

You already know that we first met because Erik was working in Switzerland, doing something for the railways. It was
autumn when I walked into this bar – Didi's or Diana's or something. I was thirsty, and there in front of me was this gorgeous
man with a thick, dark-blond beard. He was alone too, and
I spoke to him. I liked him from the start, even though I could
barely understand a word he said. It was like the words got stuck
in his beard. I kept having to ask him to speak more clearly.
He was obviously struggling, so I suggested we go outside.
I wanted to go for a walk, but he didn't. He liked being in a
crowd of men at the bar, he said, because it made him feel like
he was talking a lot, like he was talking through the mouths
of those men. That was enough for him. I thought he was so
poetic.

Verena laughed and carried on. I went to the bar the next
night too, and the next, and the days after that, although – or
really because – the bar wasn't part of my new life. I'd only been
living in Baden for a year. I had finally left my parents' world
behind me, and now this blue-collar guy was pulling me back
in. Erik was so different. He was open, pleasant in a special sort
of way. I immediately felt like I could confide in him. I was
twenty-two at the time.

Verena shoved her hands into her jacket pockets and thought.

No, I was twenty-three. Always searching for something
to cling onto, because I was so mixed up about my attraction
to women. As far as the outside world was concerned, Erik
became my husband – ten years older, this big, good-looking
guy – but really he was more of a buddy. A person I had something in common with. Living with him gave me more room

for manoeuvre. Not that we weren't also lovers. I moved in with him, into his small loft apartment.

Verena paused for a moment.

I remember very clearly the day Erik strode into my parents' house for the first time. He was holding a big bunch of flowers, at least twenty tulips. My mother stared, first at this man stooped over in the hallway so he wouldn't bump his head on the low ceiling, then at the flowers he was holding out. She couldn't believe it. My family, the whole village, they only ever really thought of him as this tall foreigner. Over dinner my father sprinkled sugar on his salad in silence. I knew he was wondering when we were getting married, and he certainly wasn't the only one. Nobody said it out loud, though, not even when I got pregnant with you.

Verena turned to face Rahel, a concentrated look that struck her with full force.

From then on, more or less everybody only had eyes for you. Erik faded into the background. But I knew my parents thought we were a disgrace.

Verena took a handkerchief from her jacket pocket and wiped her forehead.

We didn't ask each other a lot of questions. If he was going away for the weekend or when he took time off from work, he simply said: I'm going home. I accepted that by 'home' he meant whatever he saw fit. And I was glad he asked no questions when I spent the night out. When I got back to the flat, you looked tiny in his arms, Rahel, and he looked like a big kid. As though he was afraid of crushing you. Sometimes I wondered whether he was really your dad. But no one else was in the picture.

Verena fell silent.

From beneath the forest floor, roots had groped their way to the surface: scaly serpentine bodies at rest.

You didn't know Inge back then, did you? asked Rahel.

We moved to Settikon six months after you were born, Verena said. That's where things started with Inge and ended with Erik. He wasn't happy, I could tell, but he hardly ever talked about it. Settikon wasn't the right place for him. For me it was, though. I'm glad I was able to live my life there in a way that was right for me. I know it wasn't always easy for you and Fenna, and I'm sorry.

Fenna hooked her arm through Verena's.

It really wasn't all that bad, you know, she said.

Did he really go to Asia or South America? asked Rahel.

Did I say that?

Yes.

I'm sorry, I don't remember.

You can't be serious!

As I said yesterday, there was a lot of work to be done. I remember that very well, said Verena. Paper round in the morning, office in the afternoon, plus cooking, cleaning, umpteen errands to run. But I remember quiet moments too. I remember the early days with Inge, and your childish faces growing up. My two pretty girls.

And you know what I remember? asked Rahel sharply. When you burned Erik's postcard on the balcony. Your cold back as you turned and went inside without another word.

She raised her voice. You were so fucking selfish sometimes!

They were quiet as they walked on over the forest floor; Rahel felt small, like a child brimming with unutterable rage.

And you were the total fucking opposite as well, she went on, her voice shaking.

She stopped.

Who am I even talking to right now? she cried.

Fenna and Verena kept walking, until gradually their footsteps slowed.

All at once Rahel felt pleasantly heavy. Her cheeks ballooned, her whole body ballooned, she grew taller and wider, she had doubled in volume by the time Verena turned around and said: To me.

18

I *make my ground out of words, spreading out what I have: children,
milk, midges, garden, vegetables, cellar, preserves, a man, beds, cracks in
the wood, clothes, soaps, brushes, the hide, my notebook. I write on paper
dyed with calcium carbonate. I work on limestone in biro, sometimes
pencil; I write: my girl, my boy. Tremors over my skin, in my fingers.
I write my ground out of words out of books and cross the clearing. Ahead
of me, first images arise. And last.*

My first sight of you: lips astonishingly full, your head broad and round, damp dark hair tousled and your eyes closed, two deep creases either side of your nose.

You are all alone still in your world of clear amniotic fluid. You grow millimetres every day, and I watch you open-mouthed.

As though I could guess what your hands might reach for, who you might look at with your eyes.

As though I could spare you from knowing the confines of shapes and colours and names. Our house then: a waystation in your life, a memory, and myself a woman you called mother, maybe.

I build my world out of words out of books. I see Heba, the fig, I eat, and in my arms is a child. I have placed myself over my daughter like a stencil and now I see again, I draw again, I draw freehand in the air the vision of you that I had, Verena.

Mother, with your back to me, you lower the receiver, turn and smile.

Mother, crouching on the bathroom floor with a cloth in your right hand; did I make too much mess?

I turn over the flashcards of the past. Synonyms, antonyms: mother, mother. Manhater, manhater, loving, loving, confidante, confidante, absent, absent, cook, cook, working, working, breadwinner, bread-winner, lesbian, lesbian, mute, mute, slut, slut, storyteller, storyteller. Sharing, sharing. Daughter, daughter. Memory, sediment.

19

Dazed, she had boarded the train and made the journey. Despite the muddle in her head and the alcohol in her blood she had got off at the right stop and hurried past the industrial buildings, the apartment blocks and the New Apostolic Church. She had rushed as quickly as she could through the forest until she saw Boris's house, where all the lights were out. And now, at the sight of her home, she vomited at last. A pulpy flood of wine, Campari, toast, salted nuts, spaghetti bolognese, schnapps and chocolate came spasming out, landing at her feet, and she retched and heaved, gullet stinging, mouth seared, until nothing but transparent phlegm came up. Rahel awoke in bed.

Boris, hearing her outside, had gone to check and hadn't realised who it was that stood there swaying: a woman in a miniskirt and fluid-soaked blouse. She must have been a runaway, she must have been kidnapped; she must have had an accident or been confused, giving off a sweet, sharp tang of alcohol, vomit and milk.

He had stopped a few feet away and shouted at this woman: Where were you, for Christ's sake? Do you have any idea how worried I've been?

She hadn't made a single sound, nor the day after, while her empty notebook lay open by her bed.

I called the police! Boris had shouted. I called Fenna and I've been all round the forest with the kids. I checked every café in the village, every shop, every waiting room at the station, but there was no sign of you, my God, what were you thinking?

Rahel's lips had stayed shut, even when he stroked her cheeks then glared at her again a moment later; even when he set a bowl of pasta beside the bed without a word, even when he told her this was pointless now, that he was going for some fresh air with the children.

She was back, thrown again on her own resources. Boris had tried to call her thirty-one times the day she went missing, Maya twelve, and her phone, which had been under her pillow all the while, showed two unknown numbers as well.

Maya tried to reach her three more times the following day, but she didn't pick up. In the end she sent a text: Sorry for everything. I'm at home.

Then the fever came on. Gloom and brash light broke over her in waves. In those hours she was nothing but her body. Rahel looked down at herself, shivering, and gazed at her swollen, dark-red breasts; two warning lights attached to her trunk.

I'm cutting them off, I'm cutting them off, she screamed at Boris as he took her out to the car and drove her to hospital on the third day of her fever.

At the hospital they prescribed antibiotics, with the words: Just keep breastfeeding as often as possible and it will go away. And try not to get so hysterical.

20

They gathered wild garlic, dandelions and nettles. The pleasant throbbing inside Rahel had returned and lingered, trailing vague thoughts of Chris and her father as she bent down to pick the leaves and put them in a paper bag. As she stood in front of a bushy clump of nettles, an image of Boris appeared above the plants, a simple photograph, sharp contours, projected onto the landscape. Instantly the feeling of connection rose back up. She took a step towards the image, then another, and with every centimetre she moved she grew clearer and more cheerful.

They rinsed the herbs outside, in the cool gush of the stream, then dabbed them dry with a cloth. In the kitchen they chopped them into fine strips, mixed in pine nuts, salt and oil, then puréed everything. The finished pesto was decanted into glass jars and sealed.

It's like we're preserving this spring, said Fenna.

Together they went downstairs into the cellar with the fresh jars of pesto.

You're out of your mind, said Verena, inspecting the crammed shelves. You could feed an army with this lot!

Rahel let her eyes wander over the neat rows of jars and tins, the vegetables and the conserves. She started to laugh uncontrollably, bracing herself against the shelves with one hand while flapping the other in Verena's direction, as though beckoning her mother to join in.

Let's eat some, she said. As much as we can. Come on, upstairs!

It's a barbarian raid, said Fenna, reaching for a jar of pickles.

Carrying a dozen jars, they went back up the steps and placed them on the dining table in the front room: vegetables, fruit, purée, jams and pesto. Rahel fetched cutlery, some small bowls, plates and napkins.

For each jar we open, one of us is going to share a memory, she said. I'll start.

Disappearing into the kitchen, she returned with a large bottle of herbal schnapps. She poured herself a glass.

Want a sip?

Fenna and Verena both shook their heads.

Rahel opened a jar of sweet-and-sour vegetables, spooned some into the three bowls and handed one each to Fenna and Verena.

She sat mutely in front of her portion. Downing the schnapps, she poured herself another.

A girl is lying, a girl is sitting, a girl is standing, she said.

Rahel was sitting up now, speaking more quickly and firmly. A girl walks in a circle, round and round and round. From a tree hangs a curtain and behind it is a man and a woman. They're moaning and screaming and the girl doesn't know – is it love or fear or both? The girl sees the insect on her outstretched hand and the sky beyond. She keeps moving in a circle, saying one letter over and over: P, P, P, her lips are hurting. The curtain rustles and distends, trying to swallow everything. The girl plucks all the legs off the insect and hoards them, she leaps higher and higher, and now she sees the sun, but the girl has forgotten something.

Rahel stopped.

Didn't you say something about memories? asked Fenna.

Rahel took another gulp of schnapps. The glass clinked as she set it back on the table.

The girl has forgotten the balcony, she went on, and she knows she has to go back. One more time. The balcony has fallen off the house where it used to be attached. It's lying in a field, overgrown with green moss and pale-brown lichen. The girl climbs in, letting her arms dangle over the railing, and a woman appears, tall, slender and translucent. She strokes the girl's hair and face, slips her hand inside her, and disappears. The girl can sleep.

Fenna and Verena stared at Rahel in astonishment.

She raised her glass.

And now, she said, bon appétit!

Another glass of schnapps, and she forked a piece of cauliflower into her mouth.

Enjoy, girl, said Fenna.

Verena ate too, slowly chewing one piece of vegetable after another. When her bowl was empty, she pushed it slightly into the middle.

Let's have something sharp now, said Fenna, pointing at the jar of pickled ginger.

Rahel handed it to her.

Fenna placed a few slices of ginger in each bowl.

This balcony, she began, it represents something that's missing, doesn't it? Something that has yet to be defined. A gap in your landscape. I get that. I told Luc several times how much I wanted to fill in the gaps. I wanted to walk through deserted areas of landscape and bring them to life. I used to imagine running a farm or owning a little house in the countryside. And just yesterday I realised how much I hate houses. Don't take this the wrong way, Rahel, but you get so used to the walls, the dust, the hair in the drains and the people around you. You get used to yourself. To what you think you know. And to being silent. I told Luc: Sometimes I dream of gaps. And I was talking about myself.

What do you mean? asked Rahel.

I meant me, my gap. I meant I want to reach points in myself I've never touched before. I dig my finger into my cunt, I feel myself. Luc pushes his finger into it, what does he feel? I still don't really understand myself enough, and I think that's a good thing.

Fenna, are you pregnant? asked Verena.

Startled, Fenna looked at her mother.

Yes.

I've thought you might be for a while.

Are you upset I didn't say anything?

I'm sure you have your reasons.

I'm due in late autumn.

That's nice.

Fenna drummed her fingers on the table, then turned to Rahel.

Luc got in touch. He wants to see me.

Are you relieved?

I don't know. Suddenly it's all getting so real.

Rahel took her fork, held it up and let it fall it to the floor with a clatter. She bent down, picked it up and dropped it a second time.

That's what it will be like, she said. That's how real a child is.

OK, I get it, Fenna said.

Rahel bent down again and put the fork on the table. She let down her hair, skimmed her hands through it and gathered it tightly back up.

What's going on with Luc? asked Verena.

I'll tell you later, said Fenna. We were sharing stories.

You're right about hair getting everywhere, said Verena. In the corners, on the bathroom floor, in the drain, in the mashed potatoes, up my nose. Your hair, Inge's hair, my hair too. Just before you were born, Fenna, it was still long and wavy. And I remember shaving it off the day after Erik left. My head was so marvellously light all of a sudden. For ages I liked myself with short hair, until about a year ago I decided to let it grow out. I was so pleased to have chin-length hair again after all that time. But I made the decision too late. I got diagnosed with cancer and the hair had to go, once and for all. When it started falling out from the chemo, I made a paste out of cognac and egg and washed it off with that. Now I wear this red wig. Every morning I look at myself in the mirror and wonder: Why this colour? Do you think it's nice?

Bit lurid, said Rahel, but there's no chance of you being confused with someone else.

Verena smiled into space.

The girl and the woman, she said.

She turned her head and looked at Rahel.

The balcony, she persisted.

The ash from your cigarette, said Rahel.

Your little childish face.

She stroked Rahel's cheek, but said nothing else. There was only her touch, which got under Rahel's skin and spread.

Maybe your hair will grow back completely differently, she said. Blonde or black. Curly. Or like felt.

Dreads, said Verena, laughing.

Feathers, said Rahel.

I'll start clucking.

You'll grow a beak overnight.

Verena's eyes sparkled.

I'll tell you another memory, OK? she asked. It was Inge who started the whole egg thing. Just after we moved to the countryside, I was out walking you, Rahel, in the pram, when in a field outside a tiny dilapidated-looking farm we saw five cackling hens. I watched them for a while, until suddenly I got this craving for eggs. I rang the bell. It took a while to open, and then there she was, Inge. She surveyed me without a word. I stood there with my legs trembling, wanting to tell her everything. All in a rush. I'd never felt anything like it. From the very beginning it was different with her, unlike anything else I'd ever experienced. Something else closed as she opened that door. What I really wanted to ask was whether I could come inside and sit at her table, but I just pointed at the hens. She leant over the pram and smiled at you, Rahel. I went back to Erik, back to our flat in the middle of the village, with four eggs and Inge's permission to return. I hadn't moved into that flat unwillingly, mind you. Our home was clean and tidy, the way life should be. Our little family. My relationship with Inge developed slowly, gently, painstakingly, while my relationship with Erik slowly, gently, painstakingly fell apart. I always thought it would end quietly too, but I didn't count on how betrayed I would ultimately feel. The moment I knew Erik was gone forever, I realised I could never allow myself to do that. I was a mother, so I was trapped. But he was free. I struggled with that for a long time, and with Inge, too. But she hasn't left my side. I never wanted to discuss this with you. Maybe that was a mistake. Maybe not everything went as smoothly as it could have for you. But I hope you appreciate your rough edges. I hope you get more deeply knotted in yourselves and in the world and don't polish those edges away. And now, Rahel, I'd really like some of that schnapps.

Rahel got to her feet. She fetched a glass from the cupboard, put it in front of Verena and filled it. Verena took two sips.

Didn't you ever feel like just walking out? asked Rahel as she sat back down.

Sometimes I felt like throwing in the towel, yes, answered Verena. But only for a minute. After all, it's not like there was actually anything missing from my life. I had you, my work, all the good people around me, and in between all that I also had my freedom.

I wasn't sure if you'd always been into women, said Rahel. Or if it was more that you got put off men.

Women have always been my favourite. And men, men are great too.

Verena crossed her legs, a smile playing around her lips.

Reaching doggedly for the pickled mushrooms, Rahel opened the jar.

Now that, said Fenna, looks utterly disgusting.

Rahel fished some mushrooms out of the jelly-like sauce and put three on Fenna's plate.

Who wants some ham and bread to go with it?

Rahel left the living room with Verena's words still in her head. Finding freedom here and there, always on the lookout for new possibilities, picking and choosing, recombining. Speaking or not speaking. She'd had the same feeling, once, of wanting to blurt out everything at the same time – with Boris. Why hadn't she done it?

She returned with meat, bread, a bottle of red wine and two glasses. Suddenly it all felt so easy.

Just a drop?

She looked at Verena, who nodded hesitantly.

I've just thought of something, began Rahel. I was about ten years old the first time I sat down in front of the mirror, stark naked, and bent my knees. I examined myself for quite a while, from every angle I could think of. I was looking at what you called the vulva, Mum.

Rahel sat down and drank some of her wine.

I was determined to find my own word for it, so there I was, on my knees. Finally I pulled up my trousers, shocked by what I'd found between my legs. The word vagina was completely wrong, I realised that, at least, but I couldn't find the right term. Later I started using your word, just for simplicity's sake. And today I like it. Only the other day I sat down again in front of the mirror and examined myself. Imagine, I've had two kids, but I've not looked at my vulva since I was a child. The hair, the soft flesh, and I slipped my finger into the opening and it was so incredibly good.

Rahel took another sip from her glass.

That's great, said Fenna. Feels like gradually we're talking about the same thing. I've always liked examining myself like that, imagining flying around on my cunt.

Flying?

The outer lips are wings. The cunt is a little bird.

Fenna mimicked the fluttering wings of a bird with her hands; Rahel burst into a fit of snorting.

I've never used those words, she said, regaining her composure. But they really turn me on. Cunt. Take a bite out of my fig. Come and fuck.

Do you guys still have sex, you and Boris? asked Fenna.

It's been complicated since Leni.

You don't feel like it?

He does. I don't. I used to be the one who wanted it more than he did. I was always cuddling up against Boris's back, stroking his belly. I've always held back from simply saying: I want to fuck. I'm afraid he'll be disgusted, while I get hot even thinking about those words. But I could never really show him that I wanted it. Since Leni was born, suddenly he's saying it so naturally. Fuck. But it doesn't affect me anymore. Maybe I'm just jealous. Because, deep down, I always felt I needed his permission to say that word.

Rahel straightened her shoulders.

I'll get my libido back sooner or later.

We've lost so many fantastic words – we've had so many of them stolen from us! said Fenna. Viva la vulva! Hooray for cunts! I keep hearing people say things like 'down there' or 'between my legs' when they're talking about female genitalia. Or simply 'vagina', I hear that way too often. The vagina is important, sure, I've always said so, but all it is is the part of the body that connects the vulva – the external bit – to the inside. I won't let myself or anyone around me reduce the female sexual organs to this tube of mucous that isn't even visible from the outside. There's the vulva, the clitoris, the vagina, the cervix, the ovaries, all that and much more!

You're such a smartarse, laughed Rahel.

Fenna fixed her sister with a stern gaze.

I know, she said. And I've got something to say to you, too. You've got to talk to Boris. And don't mince words.

Silence.

Rahel was sitting bolt upright in her chair, one hand gripping the stem of her wine glass, the other brushing back and forth across the wooden table.

Verena cleared her throat.

Did you know, she said, that in Florence there's a square called the Piazza della Passera? Inge and I were there the year before last. We had an apérol spritz in the middle of the square. We read in the guidebook that passera can mean a female bird. And also female genitalia. They didn't quite come out and say that passera can simply be translated as cunt or pussy, but Inge knew. We laughed so hard. There we were, sitting on the Piazza della Pussy, drinking these orange drinks out of long-stemmed glasses.

A jolt swept through Rahel. The stiffness left her body, and she raised her glass at the same time as Verena.

You probably don't want to shock anybody by writing cunt or pussy in a guidebook, Rahel said with a grin, raising her glass to Verena's then putting it to her mouth.

I'd glue an explicit image of an actual cunt into the book, said Verena, who was still holding up her glass. Words are much too easily ignored.

Flower, penis, tree, vulva, slick, lick, taste, said Fenna.

Crust, said Rahel. Floor. Score. Tits, lips, hips.

And the pussy, said Fenna. Cushy, pushy.

Anyway, said Verena, the square is in the middle of an area called Santo Spirito. The Holy Ghost.

Holy fuck! Rahel blurted.

Between the legs of the Santo Spirito is the Piazza della Passera, continued Fenna. Or: please enjoy a cool apérol spritz on the Piazza della Passera, a pretty square in the middle of the holy horndog area of Florence, and look at the buildings, the winding streets, the lively hustle and bustle, the comings and goings, as the glass grows wet with condensation in your hand and your palms get damp. Lean back and enjoy!

They ate pickles, pesto with bread, sweet-and-sour courgettes, diced pumpkin and applesauce, pears and damson plums in sugar water. Eventually, Rahel stood up.

I forgot something, she said, and hurried into the cellar.

She sat down on the bottom step. For a moment she felt completely sober. Then she took out her phone and texted Boris: I miss you.

She pressed send.

Then she typed: I miss you and your eyes and your mouth and the way you speak and who you are.

Send.

I want to lay myself before you, open myself, strip my clothes off piece by piece, strip off skin after skin, and show you what's underneath. What's beyond.

Send.

I have so much to tell you.

Send.

Glad you're coming back.

Send.

Then she returned to Verena and Fenna with a big jar of pickled eggs.

I pickled them a year ago, she said, when I was about five months pregnant with Leni, and suddenly out of nowhere I didn't want to eat anything except eggs. Same thing happened when Rico was a couple of months old. So our fridge filled up. I'd have driven you nuts, Mum, with the number of eggs I brought home. We couldn't fit Boris's beer and Rico's yoghurt and the milk in there anymore. What to do with the eggs? I wondered. Preserve them.

She opened the jar and jabbed one of the eggs. It broke into several pieces.

You're pissed, said Fenna. Give it here.

She took the fork and fished an egg out of the liquid, cut it open with a knife and tried it.

Not bad.

Lovage, oregano, rosemary, said Rahel. Want one?

She looked enquiringly at Verena.

Love to. Even if I am about to burst.

Come on, said Fenna, pickles don't fill you up.

Rahel placed an egg each on Verena's and Fenna's plates, then one on her own.

Funny dessert to have after dessert, she said.

The best dessert I can imagine, said Verena.

Inside me the tectonic shifts bring about a new order. A toppling of words. Clot of blood, since childhood, the ghosts of risk. The mouth of my womb is telling me it wants to open for another child, for a word, for the world. It says: Let us meet in the new, let us put aside the images that we had and that we have. Images of my mother.

And images of Boris.

PART THREE

G*etting some distance.*

From Rico as a baby in a sling. You can barely tell where my body ends and his begins.

From Leni in my belly, knocking on the inside, still a nameless being.

Growing closer to Boris, father, husband, partner. Me on the train: crowded with passengers, mostly old. The woman next to me is dressed entirely in shades of pink. Expensive fabrics, freshly laundered. Her hair light brown, obviously dyed and straw-like, her hands wrinkled, a golden ring on her finger, a dark stone. She says: Marie looked so pretty with those earrings, such discreet make-up, that's what I want when I go.

Next stop: Romanshorn. Lake Constance on the right. Soft prattle about roses, weather, shopping. Children crying further up the train. A man of sixty odd calls over to his companion. He repeats:

    Want to get out here or what?
    Yeah.
    I don't mind.
    Let's go.
    We don't have to.

Yeah, we just have to pay our taxes and die and that's it, mutters another woman opposite.

The pink lady next to me nods.

The train stops, people get on and off; they wish each other a nice day.

A young woman and her daughter are beside me now, the girl in white Adidas shoes with purple stripes, the mother flicking through a free newspaper.

Sunny day in late spring. It was so hot yesterday that I went swimming outdoors with Boris, Rico and Leni. Astounding how busy it was: couples sunbathing, individuals and little groups in the wooden bathhouse. Behind that the area reserved for women. Elderly ladies, topless, sliding languidly into the water. Finally, the families by the kids' pool and the sandpit, dozens of children in neon UV caps digging in the sand, splashing in the water. A woman offered Rico strawberries from a large Tupperware. He looked at me queryingly. I nodded, and he pushed one into his mouth and scurried after Boris to the learner pool. I had on a grey bikini with yellow stripes. I hadn't worn it since I first met Boris. I'd taken the children swimming as infrequently as I took them to the zoo or the park or to one of those places where families lay themselves so bare that parts of their structure become apparent: what they eat at picnics, when parents tell off their children, how they talk to each other, where love handles have waxed or waned over the years. My skin gleamed white, my thighs covered by a towel; Leni slurped at my breast for the last time. My bikini top lay in the grass beside us, torn a little at the back: the fabric wasn't used to being stretched.

That was nice, said Rico on the way home. Are we coming back again tomorrow?

You and Leni and Dad, maybe.
Just us three?
Just you three.

Now I'm on the train, alone among many, alone among strangers, seventeen minutes past ten – where are all these people going? To the countryside, to the city, to shops and pharmacies? Or to festivals, like me? Music. Stages. Concerts – I like to listen. A ticket in my bag and a room booked at a hotel: Halle. I'm not back until the day after tomorrow. At home: my family. How brittle, how fragmented, how it shines and shimmers. The faces, the names. How painfully lovely.

*

When Verena left the day before yesterday, shortly before Fenna, I couldn't tell her that I'd miss her.

*

Across the border, Germany. Their countryside like ours, green and brown and the blue sky above, a river, a football pitch, billboards, a solitary linden tree, everywhere the ruffled grass. Fenna sent me a message on WhatsApp. She'd woken up bleeding heavily, was all she wrote. Didn't she say something about a stomach ache when she was at ours?

Luc getting in touch then clamming up again, that hurt her feelings. She didn't say so, but I saw how quiet she got the day before she left. I saw her lying on the deckchair outside, hands on her bare belly, the mild way she laughed when Rico carried out a jam sandwich for her on a tray. The way she barely said a word when Verena asked her about Luc, about the pregnancy, about her future with a child. An autumn baby, Fenna had emphasised again. An apple child. And with that she smiled.

Poppies on the riverbed, music in my head, on, on, repeat, doors will open on the right-hand side; the Danube.

Persist and flow; Fenna has a baby inside, in her belly, in her head. Is she sleeping next to Luc today? Is he holding her hand, whispering into her ear?

Four young people are sitting in the next row but one, speaking English. Guys, OK, everybody, I don't remember this happening.

Was he like tall?

With a hat?

I'm so sorry.

I feel so bad.

I think of Fenna, of the blood.

★

That's a great idea, said Boris, when I told him I was going to the festival alone. I needed a night away, one night in a soft hotel bed, white sheets, to fall asleep after a concert with the notes still in my head. 'Daddy Longleg'. Maybe they'd play that. A jazz festival where the band that had planted a seed in my head long ago was playing, the band that had made me write and sing about my father. I didn't know what the members looked like, how old they were. I'd never googled them. I'd only heard the singer's bright voice in my head, the driving beat, the melodic keyboard.

Why don't you stay for two nights, said Boris.

Are you trying to get rid of me? I asked.

See, where does stuff like that come from?

I don't want you getting all excited, says one of the young women.

That's so great.

I don't know how drunk you were.

We were lying on one of the deckchairs outside. Boris was holding me tightly.

Are you drifting away from me? I asked.

South-west, he answered.

Your thoughts?

Bit drunk.

How much have you had?

A few beers.

That's enough, right?

Ah, don't start. You know I need it.

★

She texted again: So much blood, what should I do, where should I go?

On the train, definitely go to the doctor. Isn't Verena there? I typed. And: I'm sorry.

Then nothing else. The landscape gliding by.

I changed trains at Frankfurt and bought a roll, eating it on the platform. A woman put a toe outside the line around the smoking zone and was scolded by her friend, a dark-haired woman with pencilled eyebrows. The bread left a sweet taste in my mouth.

Would I have begrudged Fenna this path with Luc, the path she imagined? Why don't I think it will work out with him? Both are taking what they need, Fenna as Heba, giving Luc eternal life with her fig. Although it isn't quite that easy, she knows that too. And Luc? I picture him the first time I met him, the hardness in his face. I kept my distance from the start, embarrassed by the cavalier way he treated Fenna. Bring me another coffee, will you? Come and sit on my knee. Could you just be quiet a minute?

The way Rico didn't seem to hear me when I said goodbye. He was too busy with his train set: the rails had to be connected up, the carriages joined. I told him I'd be back the day after next. He narrowed his eyes, then suddenly he was bawling, flinging his arms around my stomach. Mum, he shouted three times. I pulled his hands away and he stared at me in disbelief as I said: I'll bring you back a new CD.

Hand in hand we went downstairs, where Boris was on the sofa in the living room, holding Leni in a sling. She was asleep. I stroked her hair, again and again; it's been growing so much lately, and no one can explain the sudden tinge of red. Boris kissed me on the cheek. His lips sought mine, his tongue sliding into my mouth, electrifying me. In that moment my whole body wanted him, and he said: Let's go.

You waving on the platform, me in tears that only welled over as I turned my back and watched the train pull in. I got on. Where to? Away, then back again. Three days, nothing really, a wisp. How many days will I spend without the children? How many days have I spent without Verena? Without Erik.

Carry on, why not, to Hamburg, and board a freighter bound for Asia or South America. Find an old man in his house, where there are pictures on the walls: Rahel as a little girl in his arms. A man with nothing to say to me, who glares dumbly at the camera. What does he recall?

Or get off, take the next train back – to the home I've made, to the little house near Gesswil, to Boris's arms.

There are two old women behind me. They didn't know each other but have now bonded for the duration of the journey. One is sitting by the window, one by the aisle. Their speech is orderly: pauses between sentences, pauses between one voice and the other, sometimes longer, sometimes shorter. Sometimes there's nothing to be heard for several minutes. Their topics are where to change trains and provisions. How far they are from their children. One woman lives in Konstanz, with children in Leipzig and Kassel, while the other lives in Freiburg with her children quite close by.

Oh no, that's the last thing I need, I dropped my yoghurt, one of them suddenly says a little louder.

Could have happened to anybody, responds the other one.

Sorry?

Could have happened to anybody.

We ate the pickles and preserves, we drank some wine – a whole bottle. That's not good for you, I told Verena, are you allowed?

The doctors aren't my mother, she had answered, snorting with laughter. She looked like a disobedient little girl.

Don't worry, she said a moment later, I'm optimistic. I'll get better. I caught a shadow flit across her face and hugged her. It felt strange, being so drunk and knowing that the impulse to hug her was dishonest. Or was it the other way around – was the dishonest part my impulse to question the hug?

Next morning when I told her about it, Fenna just shook her head. Verena, Boris and the children were still asleep and we were arm in arm outside, waiting for the sun to rise.

Boris had brought the kids back the night before. They'd had a nice time, he said, and Rico agreed.

Leni drank, her lips pursed around my nipple, comfortably this time, to my surprise, and yet I wasn't upset knowing it would be the last. I'd been weaning her for ages. She stretched out her little arms and I touched each and every finger, a little shamefaced, but only because I hadn't quite sobered up yet, and I knew there would be a trace of the alcohol in the milk.

Verena, Fenna and I had finished our giddy lunch about three hours earlier. In the middle of all the exuberance, I'd got up and staggered over to the sofa, flopped onto the plush cushions and said: I'll leave it there, good night.

I'd heard Fenna and Verena laughing, glasses clinking and plates being put away, then I slipped into a dream, but I was so far gone, so deep into myself, that I remembered nothing at all when I woke up two hours later with a pounding headache.

Verena and Fenna weren't in the living room. Instead I heard Boris's car, footsteps on the gravel, the front door opening, and suddenly Leni was on top of me and Rico beside me and Boris's hand in my hair. I could tell from the way he was looking at me that he knew I was drunk. He said nothing, and in his saying nothing I sensed our bond, sensed it in the open look he fixed on me, and beyond that the years we had lived through side by side, and I felt again how much I had to say to him in the coming days and weeks. I mentioned something else, too, as Fenna and I stood outside the next morning, dazzled by the rising sun. That I was afraid sometimes Boris might be too good for me, like Chris had been. And that he, unlike Chris, might realise that and leave.

Boris loves you, said Fenna. You can see that from a mile away. Now for god's sake, when you feel your mind going round in circles, try to take a step back.

She would be leaving the next day, she informed us that morning, taking the train back to Zurich to meet Luc and hopefully get things sorted.

After Verena got up, around half-ten, she called Inge on the phone in the corridor and told her enthusiastically about the pickled eggs we'd eaten the day before, about the patch of marsh, about Fenna's pregnancy. I shut the kitchen door and turned up the radio.

Inge says hi. She's picking me up tomorrow, Verena announced when she walked into the kitchen fifteen minutes later.

But you've only just arrived, I said.

My next hospital appointment is in two days, didn't I say? We'll see each other again soon, she added, smiling at me – the smile not of a mother but a confidante.

*

Dozed off just after Leipzig and had the same dream as the night we opened the jars. I was fumbling through the house with the dark corridor, turning handles, stepping into empty room after empty room, until at last, behind one of the doors, was Verena. Every piece of her was exaggeratedly huge. She was naked, and all at once the parts of her body began to wander; they shifted around her torso, which was pulsing heavily, and I watched agape as she rotated, fingers and toes, individual hairs, arms and legs, lips, wrinkles and cheeks; everything was in motion, and when I tried to take hold of my own left arm I felt something soft. Looking down, I saw that my limbs were rotating too, at a leisurely, synchronised pace. I leant back. And there was music.

217

I woke with a jolt, drool trickling from my mouth. The sensation of movement was still in my body, and the echo of those peculiar sounds. The landscape was still rolling past. I sat very still and looked out of the train window. It wasn't long before we reached Halle.

★

Arrived. Went from the station to the hotel on foot. Friendly receptionist, small clean room. I put my suitcase on the luggage rack, as yet unpacked. What did I really need for such a short stay? All I took out was the book about the last ancient forest, flicked through a few pages.

Why are you lugging that around? It's much too heavy, Boris had said when he saw me packing the day before.

I'm just interested, I said. Something to put in the wheelie case.

Thinking of Fenna, far away, but it touches me, her blood, and I'm afraid she's lost the child.

★

Calcium carbonate, chalkstone, lime. Calcium in bone, lime in carbonic acid; connections are made, lime is scattered: it stabilises the acidity, they say, and makes the plants grow.

Lime in the walls of our cellar, in the pages of the book in my hand.

And the grass in the clearing feeds on humus and lime.

★

I rest before I head out to the festival, lying down for just a minute. I could write and keep on writing, the first melodies appearing in my head. What I know now: it's not a house of my own I need but a roof, a place to write, to be, to sing again, to let what happens happen, walls around me, to let

218

what arises arise. The barn near the forest, maybe. I could insulate it with Boris, do it up, get myself settled in there all alone: my table, my chair, my notes, my scores; walls papered with articles, with ideas. A place to focus, to summon, to work, and perhaps at last, when I'm able, to find myself again. I'll come back to the city and I'll sing. I have time.

Thank you to

Francesco, because you're always hovering above every text,
Werner, for your faith in this novel,
Angela, for your help polishing,
Julia, for your enthusiasm,
Mithu, for your book *Vulva*,
Karsten, for your perspective on the world, on the text and the way it moves,
Andi, for the way you helped me think things through, accompanying me from the beginning,
Ilias and Hella, simply for coming to us,
and, of course: my mother.